"IT IS FAST-MOVING AND OFTEN DOWNRIGHT FUNNY."
—*New York Times*

Eddie Ryan felt exhilarated for getting through his First Confession so smoothly—until later when he realized he had quite inadvertently . . . LIED!

"Neither Father O'Reilly nor my classroom nun had told us what happened to someone who lied in Confession. Probably no one had ever done it before so there wasn't even a rule to cover it.

"The phone rang. I knew it had to be the priest who had heard my confession He had just found out that I had lied in confession and was calling my mother to tell her that I was being expelled from St. Bastion school and excommunicated from the Church . . . and the country, just for starters."

Acknowledgments

Randy. Margo Powers, for that night at the roller rink. Gay and Dr. Joseph V. Gioioso for their contributions. Dr. Martion J. Maloney of Northwestern University, John Fink of the Chicago Tribune Magazine, and Bill Wright for both their professional and personal assistance.

ATTENTION: SCHOOLS AND CORPORATIONS

WARNER books are available at quantity discounts with bulk purchase for educational, business, or sales promotional use. For information, please write to: SPECIAL SALES DEPARTMENT, WARNER BOOKS, 666 FIFTH AVENUE, NEW YORK, N.Y. 10103.

**ARE THERE WARNER BOOKS
YOU WANT BUT CANNOT FIND IN YOUR LOCAL STORES?**

You can get any WARNER BOOKS title in print. Simply send title and retail price, plus 50¢ per order and 50¢ per copy to cover mailing and handling costs for each book desired. New York State and California residents add applicable sales tax. Enclose check or money order only, no cash please, to: WARNER BOOKS, P.O. BOX 690, NEW YORK, N.Y. 10019.

John R. Powers

The Last Catholic in America

A Fictionalized Memoir

WARNER BOOKS

A Warner Communications Company

*To my parents,
June R. and John F. Powers,
without whose love
I would not have been possible*

WARNER BOOKS EDITION

Copyright © 1973 by John R. Powers
All rights reserved.

Published by arrangement with Saturday Review Press

Portions of this book have appeared in slightly different form in *Chicago* magazine, the *Chicago Tribune Sunday Magazine*, *Scouting* magazine, and the *Houston Post*, in 1970, 1971, and 1972.

Warner Books, Inc.
666 Fifth Avenue
New York, N.Y 10103

A Warner Communications Company

Printed in the United States of America

First Warner Books Printing: December, 1982

10 9 8 7 6 5 4

Contents

I	Because	7
II	According to My Permanent Records	13
III	Confession	25
IV	Father O'Reilly	49
V	Some Great Moments in Sloppy Scouting	70
VI	The Nuns	81
VII	Lent	94
VIII	Bapa and the New York Yankees	108
IX	Dirty Shirt Andy	117
X	Felix the Filth Fiend Lindor	125
XI	Blah on the Altar Boys	147
XII	Sister Edna	165
XIII	Eighth Grade: Top of the Bottom	180
XIV	The Sex Talk	197
XV	Finale	207
XVI	SWANK	211

I Because

Q. 150. Why did God make you?
A. God made me to know Him, to love Him and to serve Him in this world, and to be happy with Him for ever in the next.

> Question 150 from the
> Baltimore Catechism

Morning flight. Cross-country from New York with but one thought in mind: to sell a few million paper cups to a lavatory firm in Los Angeles.

Talking to the fellow next to me, a law student from Harvard University. It is the usual pitter-patter conversation that often ferments between passengers of adjoining seats: dribblings of dialogue spaced by half hours of silent negligence.

I ask him where he's from.

"Pittsburgh," he replies.

"Oh," I say. That's all I can think of to say about Pittsburgh. "Oh." But it's the type of inquiry that must be reciprocated. He complies somewhat blandly.

"And you?"

"Chicago."

"Oh." He knows as much about Chicago as I do about Pittsburgh.

I ask him if he knows anyone from Chicago. I say it as if I'm on a first-name basis with all four million of the city's inhabitants.

"Only one person," he says, "a gentleman who used to be a night security guard at my father's department store. His name was . . . ah . . ." He looks up at the ceiling of the plane for the answer. "Ah, Alex Rummersfold, I believe."

"Alex Rummersfold! I know him!" I am almost shouting. Whenever I get excited, I always talk louder than I should. The Harvard law student, who is sitting next to the window, kind of turns his back on me and begins looking out at the cloudless sky.

A stewardess walking by is somewhat startled by my verbal explosion. She stares at me vacantly for a moment, then smiles weakly and moves on. I'm sure that if my head had just fallen off, she would have done the same thing. Stewardesses are like that.

"Alex Rummersfold," I say quietly to myself, "Jesus Christ, I forgot all about him." I turn in my seat toward the Harvard law student. "He's a short, squatty guy with huge shoulder blades, right?"

The Harvard law student continues to gaze out the window. "Yes, as I recall," he says.

"And he had a very odd, disgusting odor about him, right?"

That brings the Harvard law student away from his window. "Why yes, yes he did."

"That's because he has overdeveloped armpits. He's always smelled like that. He even smelled like that on his first day of school. He was the only six-year-old I knew who had fully mature sweat glands. He was an altar boy, too. Used to serve Friday night novenas all the time."

I relate the facts of Alex Rummersfold smugly. It's always a pleasure to drop a little history on the ignorant.

The Harvard law student isn't impressed. He goes back to staring out the window.

Thirty thousand feet over Ohio and thoughts of Alex Rummersfold don't mix very well in one's head so I try to think of other things. But it doesn't work. My mind keeps drifting back to Alex Rummersfold, hundreds of other people as weird as him including me, and that world we all share together.

By the time the plane reaches Chicago for a stopover, I am more interested in tracing my umbilical cord back to its origin than in sticking some guy in Los Angeles with two million four-ounce paper cups.

Taking a cab from O'Hare Airport to the far South Side of Chicago. The cab is approaching a small hill that is topped by cemeteries on either side of the street. As the cab begins crawling up the hill, I yell at the cab driver to stop.

"Right here?" he asks.

"Right here." I hand him the fare, climb out of the cab, and begin walking up the remainder of the hill. I don't dare go into my old neighborhood in a cab. In all the years I lived there, I never once saw a cab on one of its streets.

It is a good day to be alive in Chicago. I have never been a big fan of Chicago's weather. The city's winters are unbelievably cold and piled with snow. Between the frigidity of winter and the torrid heat of summer are two days called spring. But Chicago's autumns make up for all of it. They are cool days with clear complexions, flavored by crispy brown leaves and mellowed by a summer-aged sun. Today is such a day.

Looking through the wrought-iron fence as I approach the top of the hill. Grave markers and ground alike are speckled with leaves, many turned brown by the eons of summer.

There are a few newly dug graves. One is so fresh that leaves have yet to fall upon it.

An older friend of mine once told me that although you may live in many places, "home" will always be the one you grew up in. As I reached the top of the hill, I realize that he is right. Below me lies the main street of my old neighborhood.

It's a different neighborhood than most, if for no other reason than the fact that more than half of its inhabitants are dead and have been for years. Although the neighborhood is legally part of Chicago, it is isolated from the rest of the city by grave markers and evergreens. The area is entirely surrounded by cemeteries, seven of them to be exact. The neighborhood is named after the largest of these cemeteries. Seven Holy Tombs.

Seven Holy Tombs was originally a small town that was annexed into the city of Chicago sometime during the 1920s. The founder of Seven Holy Tombs was supposedly a gravedigger. But it wasn't until the late 1940s and early 1950s that the area really began to grow.

The men who came to Seven Holy Tombs were those who had fought, and won, World War II and who had used the G.I. Bill to buy their homes. Their wives were girls who had spent a few years after high school working for the telephone company and were now content to grind out the rest of their existences as mothers and housewives.

During those years, the white frame two-flats and chocolate brown brick bungalows of Seven Holy Tombs supported two V.F.W. halls, a Moose lodge, a Knights of Columbus chapter, seven music stores all of which exclusively specialized in teaching the accordion, a three-story hobby shop, four dime stores, two custard stands, the world's largest Little League organization, a dozen gas stations, and about four thousand corner food stores.

Although most of the men of Seven Holy Tombs worked in other parts of Chicago, the vast majority of residents thought you needed a visa in order to get out of the neighborhood for more than one day at a time. It was customary for the natives, upon reaching puberty, to marry the girl next door and then move two blocks away. We children of Seven Holy Tombs believed that the edge of the earth lay two blocks beyond the cemeteries. Most of the adults felt that it was somewhat farther than that.

The young couples who had come to Seven Holy Tombs in the late 1940s and early 1950s were part of the fuse that ignited the postwar baby boom. Long engagements were their only form of birth control and that didn't always prove successful either. Through their endeavors, Seven Holy Tombs became the fastest-growing community in the country. It was during this time of her adolescence that I, and thousands like me, were born and grew older in Seven Holy Tombs.

Then, there were two major religions in the world, Catholic and "Public." Catholics went to St. Bastion Grammar School, had long summer vacations, had to get off the sidewalks when a Public kid told them to since the sidewalks belonged to the Publics, and were constantly yelled at by adults who would say, "I expected better behavior from you Catholic kids, with all those nuns watching over you."

Publics went to Seven Holy Tombs Public School, had shorter summer vacations, were often subjected to "what can you expect from Public school kids" glares from adults, and went to a number of different churches in the neighborhood, which, according to the Catholics, were all the same anyway.

I notice few changes as I walk down the main street. It's a quarter to one. Almost the end of lunch period. Kids are streaming out of the various dime stores, their arms loaded down with packs of loose-leaf paper, pencil sharpeners, and new, unblemished notebooks.

In many of the boys' eyes, you can see that good old September enthusiasm. "Yes sir, this year is going to be different. I'm going to do my homework every day as soon as I get home from school. And no goofing around either. This is the year I show them what kind of student I can really be." Such enthusiasm inevitably dies within two weeks of the current campaign.

Some of their faces look familiar. Probably younger brothers and sisters of kids I grew up with.

Since I'm heading in the same direction, I walk along with them, but my step is not as fast as theirs. I don't have to be in my classroom before the bell rings.

With their accelerated pace, they shortly desert me. By the time I reach the St. Bastion parish complex, which includes the school, convent, the old church, which has been converted into classrooms, the new church, and the rectory, the school bell has rung. The playground is clear. The streets are no longer soaked with sound.

Directly across from St. Bastion is the neighborhood's major park, named quite appropriately Seven Holy Tombs Park. Being a baseball fanatic, I spent a good part of my youth chasing grounders and fly balls, most of which evaded me, across its various diamonds. With the kids in school, the park is virtually empty except for an occasional young mother pushing a baby carriage and a few old men cluttering up some of the park benches.

I get a long drink of water from the fountain, then pick out an empty bench that overlooks the park. Resting my arms along the back of the bench and stretching my crossed legs, getting all the wrinkles out. Relaxing while my body saturates the easy breathing of Seven Holy Tombs. Thinking.

II According to My Permanent Records

I didn't say good-bye to all my imaginary friends or do anything stupid like that before I went off to my first day of school. Not that I didn't have imaginary friends. At that time I had two, Joe Brown and Pete Brown. By the time I was fifteen, I had forty imaginary friends. I still hang around with a few of them.

Joe Brown was the bartender in the upstairs bathroom. Joe was the owner and Pete was his assistant. Pete Brown got his own place when we put in a bathroom downstairs.

The only place I ever sat long enough to do any serious thinking was in the bathroom. Sometimes it's easier to do serious thinking if you have someone to talk things over with. Not all the time because it's nice to be alone, too. But sometimes.

After watching all those Sunday afternoon Westerns with their sympathetic bartenders, more and more often Joe Brown would just happen to be in my bathroom when I was there. Sometime later, Pete Brown started coming around to help Joe out. After a while, I started running into Joe Brown and Pete Brown all over the house. Gradually, more imaginary friends kept coming to stay. "Friends" really isn't the proper word to use. I didn't like all of them. Bill Doodle, for instance, was a very tough guy to get to know and an impossible person to get along with. Most of them were okay, though.

It was kind of nice having all those people around. The house was like a town in itself. The upstairs hall was sometimes a street and sometimes the hallway of the hotel many of us lived in. The stairs emptied out into the living room, which, with the dining room, was the rest of the neighborhood. The kitchen wasn't anything because one of my parents or my older sister was in there most of the time. Imaginary friends and family don't mix.

I would have never considered saying good-bye to my imaginary friends before I went to school that first morning. They were adults and so was I. Like any kid I might be a cowboy one day and the next day be a major-league ballplayer and they would change right along with me. But we were always adults. So why the hell would a bartender like Joe Brown care about some kid starting school?

With a quart of hair oil seeping through my fifty-cent haircut from Angelo's Barbershop, the clip-on bow tie gouging my Adam's apple with every swallow, the suspenders constantly slipping off the three-dollar corduroy pants that scraped and scratched with every step, three unsharpened pencils wrapped in my fist, and my feet encased in Buster Brown shoes "Made Just for You," I stumbled along the streets of Seven Holy Tombs, following the early morning school crowd to St. Bastion Catholic Grammar School, wondering what God had in store for me.

St. Bastion school had no guidance counselors, televisions, gym, school nurse, faculty room, cafeteria, or field trips. St. Bastion's had classrooms. Lots of them. And each classroom had kids. Lots of them. Through the combined efforts of the parents of St. Bastion's, the parish had the largest student body of any elementary school in the city of Chicago.

A nun stood in front of the large red double doors, her arms folded and her eyes peering down at me as I cautiously began to climb, for the first of many thousands of times, the steps of St. Bastion school.

I had met nuns a few times before when I had gone to Sunday mass with my parents. The nuns were sweet to me, then. Hugging me and saying what a sweet little fellow I was and all of that. They probably just said that because I was with my parents. Nuns are always very nice to you when you're with your parents. But if you're alone, look out.

"You, what grade you in?"

"I'm not in any grade, Str, I'm just starting school today."

"Hey, what are you? Some kind of wise guy? Downstairs in the basement with the other first graders."

The walls of the school basement were lined with smooth yellow brick. At the back of the basement was a stage with the curtain closed. The curtain was crowded with squares of advertisements advocating the patronage of local businesses. "Georgi's Jewelry Shop—When you think of Mother, your priceless jewel, think of Georgi, he's a real gem, too." "Don's Donut Shop, food good for the HOLE family." "Everrest Cemetery, We care. Free water cans."

A couple of hundred wooden and metal folding chairs had been set up in front of the stage with a space left in the center of them for an aisle. All the boys were on one side and all the girls were on the other. Angelo the barber had done a good week's business. He had even got some of the girls.

Everyone was sitting as if they had been painted into their folding chairs. The nuns swished along in their black and white habits, patrolling the outskirts of the chairs. No one talked.

A few minutes later, all the nuns began mumbling, "Good morning Father, good morning Father, good morning Father." Down the center aisle came a huge, balding, black-cassocked priest with a bloated belly so big it was outdistancing his head to the stage by two or three feet. His hands clasped each other behind his back, in silent agreement that there wasn't enough room for them up front with all that abdominal flesh.

He didn't answer the nuns but simply nodded in their direction as he inched up the aisle, slowly shifting the weight from one foot to the other. The nod seemed to be enough for the nuns. They went nuts over it.

If it had been a Bing Crosby movie, the priest would have been smiling and he would have said, "Greetings, children. It's certainly nice to see all your happy faces today. My name is Father O'Reilly and I would like to welcome you to St. Bastion Grammar School. We have a lovely school here, which I'm sure you will enjoy. We at St. Bastion's believe that children should study hard, pray hard, and play hard, though not necessarily in that order." Then he'd throw in a few phony "heh heh heh's" and we'd all phony "heh heh heh" him right back. Then he'd say, "I'm sure if you listen to the good sisters, obey the rules, and cooperate with your classmates, you will come to love St. Bastion school almost as much as it loves you."

That's not the way it was. Father O'Reilly didn't introduce himself. He didn't have to. Through his years of self-sacrifice, hard work, determination, Hell-preaching, and pure intimidation, parishioners had come to fear Father O'Reilly even more than they feared God. Although we first graders believed there was a God, we KNEW there was a Father O'Reilly.

He didn't smile. He didn't "heh heh heh" us and we didn't "heh heh heh" him back. His actual talk took about three dozen words and lasted less than thirty seconds.

First, Father O'Reilly led us through about ten minutes of prayers, "Hail Marys," "Our Fathers," "Glory Be's," the usual stuff. Then he said to us,

"Obey the nuns and you won't get into any trouble. Now, I don't want to hear a sound when you leave this basement. And remember, from now on, everything you do for the rest of your life goes down on your permanent records."

After another ten minutes of prayers, we lined up, boys on the right side, girls on the left, and filed out of the basement to our classroom upstairs. Without making a sound.

My first-grade classroom had eighty-five kids in it. The nun, Sister Eleanor, spent half that first day bragging how she had over ninety kids the year before. Since at the time I couldn't count past four, neither number impressed me.

Sister Eleanor repeated Father O'Reilly's warning: everything that we did from this day forward would be etched eternally in our permanent records. She told us about how some former graduate of St. Bastion Grammar School had applied for a very important job in a steel company somewhere downtown. Sister Eleanor said that the prospective employer called the school and asked the principal to check the guy's permanent records and see how well the guy did in first grade, especially in Reading. We believed her.

Sister Eleanor also informed us that God did not like people who chewed gum in school, talked in line, or who insisted on going to the bathroom more than five times a day.

There were two other first-grade classrooms but the one I was in was a split classroom, half first graders and half second graders. In a few weeks it became apparent that Sister Eleanor felt the world of academia lay in rows four through eight, the rows of the second grade. She was always yelling at more of us than of them and she was always slugging more of us than them.

It must be admitted that, in fact, the second graders

did have a lot of class. Sister Eleanor would tell them to take out their English workbooks and they would know which book to take out. She'd tell them to take out their catechisms and they'd know which book that was, too. Instead of buckles, many of them wore tie shoes. They had to be taken to the washroom only four times a day. Vomiting among the second graders was a rarity.

On the first grade side of the room, someone was always goofing it up. We'd be lucky if we got through morning prayers without one of us getting clouted. Richard Dumple most often messed things up.

At the beginning of morning prayers, when he began making the sign of the cross, his finger tips stood a fifty-fifty chance of landing either on his forehead or in his eyes.

Usually a kid who constantly gets in trouble goes out of his way for it, at least in the beginning. Not Richard Dumple. He was different from the rest of us kids and we knew it, though we weren't quite sure in what way. He was very hairy. A few years later, he would be the only fourth grader with a five o'clock shadow.

In a class of only thirty or forty kids, you'll usually find a couple who are social outcasts and have no friends for one reason or another. But in a class of eighty-five, there are so many kids that even the weirdos have other weirdos to hang around with. But no one was as weird as Richard Dumple so he always ate lunch alone, walked home alone, or did whatever he was doing, alone.

It wasn't until I was in high school that I realized the reason Richard Dumple was different from the rest of us kids was that he was emotionally disturbed. And it wasn't until a few years later that I realized it was the other way around.

In Catechism class we memorized the answers to such questions as "Who is God?" "Who made the world?" and "What is man?" We were learning to "defend" our faith though no one ever bothered to tell us who was attacking it.

The answer to the question "Where is God?" was "Everywhere." Sister Eleanor, my first-grade nun, loved to remind us of the fact.

"You may be able to fool your parents," she'd tell us, "and sometimes even the good sisters. But never God. He is everywhere. He sees everything. He hears everything. No matter where you go, God is watching you. Remember, children, you can never put anything over on God because HE is everywhere, everywhere, everywhere."

Besides being under God's constant surveillance, Sister Eleanor told the class that each one of us had his own personal guardian angel who had been assigned by God to do nothing but watch every move that was made by the kid whom he was told to guard. I already had double coverage and I hadn't even reached the age of reason yet.

On the days that Sister Eleanor was feeling a little fruity, she'd tell us to sit on one side of our desk seats so that our guardian angels would have room to sit down. We'd do it, too. We were as crazy as she was.

Life at St. Bastion Grammar School quickly settled into a routine that varied little for the eight years I was there. The mornings would start off with Catechism followed by Math, more commonly called Arithmetic. Then English, Reading, and right before lunch, Spelling. Spelling period was held just before lunch because it wasn't that important so we could always cut it short if the necessity arose. History and Geography were in the afternoon.

We didn't have all those subjects in the first grade,

of course. All we did that year was try to remember how to get back and forth to school.

Reading period at St. Bastion's was always good for a fair amount of groin-tugging. I groin-tugged a lot during Reading period mainly because the nuns would never let you know exactly when you were going to be called on.

Normally a nun would tell a kid to stand and read a few lines from his reader out loud. After he finished, she'd ask the next kid in the row to do the same thing and so on down the row.

On occasion, however, the nun would suddenly ask a kid on the other side of the room to start reading, hoping she'd discover that he wasn't paying attention and had lost his place.

Actually, it wasn't a case of not paying attention that would cause you to lose your place but the fact that even the dumbest person could read faster silently than the kid who was standing up and reading out loud. To protect yourself from being caught off guard, you would teach your finger to read. As the kid read out loud, your finger would travel along the page of the book at the appropriate speed, underlining the words that were being read. Meanwhile, your eyes could race ahead a few pages to reveal the end of the story. If you were suddenly called on to read, your finger would save you.

The nuns always aimed such unexpected maneuvers at certain kids and never at a sugar cube such as Mary Kenny.

Mary Kenny was the top bootlicker in my class, managing to hold the title against all sorts of competition for the entire duration of grammar school. When attendance was taken each morning, she was the one who would answer "present" instead of "here." There were other teacher's pets but she was *the* teacher's pet. Mary Kenny had such a nauseating smile that she could turn your mouth inside out with disgust. Mary Kenny always sat in the front seat nearest the door, ostensibly because she was short (most bootlickers are short) and had to sit in a front-row seat in order to see the blackboard. The real reason was because, sitting in the seat closest to the door, Mary Kenny was the "natural" one to send on all errands. And if there was a fire, she could be the first one out the door. St. Bastion's could afford to lose a few ordinary kids. The school had too many anyway. But you could never have too many Mary Kennys.

All the bootlickers were like Mary Kenny. Girls, short, with very soft voices. I felt sorry for this one girl, Alice Blazer. You could tell she wanted to be a teacher's pet. Most of the girls did. But Alice Blazer was a very tall girl. She never had a chance. She was just too tall to put in a front seat.

About every two months we spent an hour in the afternoon doing Art or Music. It wouldn't have bothered me if we never had Art or Music. I never liked Art. During Art class, I always ended up sitting next to Virginia Leer, who ate her crayons and then got the runs in four different colors.

I like to sing but not the songs we sang at St. Bastion's. All we ever sang about was the Virgin Mary, except around Christmas when we sang about the Infant Jesus, too. We used to sing songs like "Queen of the May." "O Mary we crown thee with blossoms today, queen of the angels, queen of the May. . . ." Singing that kind of stuff for eight successive years can get to you.

Singing, like most things at St. Bastion's, was for the girls. The nuns always sang the songs at least twelve octaves too high for any boy. Whenever we boys tried to sing that high, it sounded like a hoe was being dragged across our throats. The major cause of hernias at St. Bastion's was "Queen of the May."

St. Bastion's believed in lines. In the morning, we came into school in a line and in the afternoon we left school in a line. We went to the washrooms, the playground, the coatroom, and up to the blackboard in line. If you felt like throwing up, there was a line for that, too. One was rarely allowed to walk around unless he was looking at the back of someone else's head. There were patrol boys stationed every ten feet who made sure we stayed in line and there were always the nuns hanging over us, daring us not to stay in line.

Lines were usually made up of double rows that were segregated: boys on the right side, girls on the left. It was considered capital punishment to put a person in the row of the opposite sex.

St. Bastion Grammar School was eight years of meandering through workbooks, praying, writing English essays that no one read, listening to the Pope on the radio, praying, standing up and telling the nun why you didn't do your homework, the excuse usually falling into one of five categories: "I forgot what the assignment was," "I left it at home," "My little brother ate it," "I can't find it," and "Uh," doing arithmetic on the blackboard and trying not to screech the chalk or trying to screech the chalk depending on the situation, coming up with nickels of mission money, praying, raising your hand to go to the washroom even though you didn't have to go—you just wanted to get out of your lousy desk for a while—making a hurried sign of the cross under orders of your nun because an ambulance siren wailed by the school, praying, reading from your book out loud to the class, praying, and watching the clock crawl around to three o'clock and summer. All of it, we were warned, went on our permanent records.

One day in the first months of first grade, I was walking home from school with Mike Depki. Depki was the only kid in the first grade who wore his hair in a "Detroit," a crew cut on top and long hair combed back on the sides. He lived at the end of my block in a large, clumsy brown frame house that looked like an old farmhouse. According to the neighborhood oral tradition, that's exactly what it was at one time, a farmhouse. Supposedly, the Depki family owned the entire neighborhood when it was still farmland. The only reason, claimed the oral tradition, that the Depki family didn't become wealthy after selling all the land for development was that they drank up all the profits. Since Seven Holy Tombs has never been worth more than a six-pack, it wouldn't have taken much drinking.

There were dozens of people in the Depki family, maybe even hundreds. They all lived in that one farmhouse. No one knew how many Depkis there actually were because the family was never seen together. Since there were so many of them living in the old farmhouse, they had to do everything in shifts.

At different times of the day, certain Depkis would be in the house eating and sleeping while other Depkis would be outside working or doing whatever they did. On blistering August afternoons, when the air was too hot even to breathe, Mike Depki would be the only kid on the street simply because it was his shift not to be in the house.

Mike Depki lived on Pepsis and Hostess Twinkies. He was every mother's example to her child of what not to eat. Yet Depki was the strongest kid in the neighborhood. And that was before the sixteen-ounce bottle.

No one in the Depki family had ever finished high school. An upper-grade nun told Mr. Depki, at the only parent-teacher conference that he had ever shown up for, that she was sorry to tell him that she thought he had a socially maladjusted child in his family. Mr. Depki said he thought so, too. He asked her if she knew which one it was.

Mike Depki had a very logical mind, which was one reason why he did so poorly in school. He was one of those guys who in class was a nominal nitwit but the moment he cleared the school door, he became the neighborhood Nietzsche.

On this particular afternoon, both Depki and I had been kept after school. I for not doing my homework and Depki for being Depki. He was telling me about the conversation he had had with one of his older brothers—the one who worked as a butcher during the day and as a bail bondsman at night.

"My brother says that the first four years of grammar school are a waste of time," said Depki. "All they teach you to do is to read and write and do arithmetic. According to my brother, you don't need any of that stuff until you're at least ten. Right?" Depki looked at me for confirmation.

"Right, Mike," I said. I didn't know what he was driving at, but I wasn't about to disagree with him. As I have mentioned, Mike Depki was the strongest kid in the neighborhood and like most intellectuals, he didn't tolerate dissent from his views. Depki continued.

"Remember how Eleanor tried to tell us if we studied hard we'd be able to read street signs, be able to count our change from the store, and be able to write letters to our friends."

"Yeah, I remember that, Mike."

"It kinda made sense to me at the time. But last night I told my brother what she said and he said that was a lot of shit."

That Depki sure was intelligent. He talked just like my father.

" 'Look, Mike,' my brother says to me, 'you know the names of the streets for four blocks in each direction and that's as far as you're allowed to go anyway.

24

After that, you deserve to get lost. And what change do you have to count from the store? Twinkies and Pepsis are a dime each. You don't have to count a dime. You see a dime. And as far as writing letters to your friends, that's a lot of shit, kid. You haven't got a friend that lives more than five doors away. Why the hell would you want to write them a letter.' Then my brother puts his arm around my shoulder and he says to me, 'Mike, why don't you skip school until you're ten and then see if it's any use to you. Speaking from my own personal experience, I really can't see why you need those first four years.' You see, Ryan," Depki said to me, "these first four years are a waste of time."

It was the only instance I can recall where Mike Depki's mind went astray. The first four years of grammar school weren't a waste of time. The first eight were.

According to my permanent records.

III Confession

It was in second grade that Father O'Reilly, the pastor of St. Bastion Church, came into our classroom to tell us about Confession. We knew something unusual was about to happen. Father O'Reilly was always the bearer of extraordinary news.

"You are now," he began, "seven years old and have reached the age of reason. Before you reached this age of reason, you were incapable of committing sin. Now, at the age of seven, you can totally comprehend right from wrong. You are capable of committing any and all kinds of sins. The week after next, you will be receiving the sacrament of Penance, which is another word for Confession. The following Sunday, you will make your First Holy Communion. Sister here will instruct you as to how to conduct yourself in Confession and Holy Communion. You better not make any mistakes."

Our nun first told us that there were two kinds of sin: Venial and Mortal. A venial sin was a minor offense against God and included such things as disobeying your parents, lying, stealing an item of small worth, deliberately not doing your homework, or not brushing after meals.

Although venial sins didn't have to be told in Confession, it was a very good idea to do so because by confessing them in Confession, we'd cut down the time we'd have to spend in Purgatory for them.

Venial sins, Sister said, were like nails in our souls. Confession pulled the nails out but there were still holes left in our souls. Purgatory took care of the holes. But if we didn't confess the venial sins in Confession, we'd have to spend an even longer time in Purgatory while the nails were being taken care of.

Then there was Mortal Sin. A mortal sin was a very serious offense against God and included such actions as missing mass on Sunday, swearing, stealing something of extreme value, divorce, murder, and eating meat on Friday.

Although it was a good idea to tell our venial sins in Confession as it would cut down our time in Purgatory, it wasn't absolutely necessary. Venial sins alone couldn't send us to Hell. But if we died with just one unconfessed mortal sin on our souls, that was the ball game. We'd go straight to Hell.

The confessional, said Sister, consisted of three attached closetlike rooms, all in a row. The middle closet, where the priest sat and listened to our sins, had a window on each side that opened into each of the closets next to it. The reason there were closets on both sides of the priest's closet was because one person could be telling his sins to the priest while the person in the other closet could be organizing his sins in order to be ready for the priest when the priest came to his window.

There was no light in the confessionals. We would be able to see nothing except perhaps the small crucifix that would be hanging above the window. Neither we nor the priest would be able to see through the window as there was a darkened screen across it. We would be able to hear only one another.

The priest would slide a wooden panel across one window in order to guarantee privacy to the person at the other window who was about to begin confessing his sins. When we heard the wooden panel sliding back from our window, we were to begin telling the priest our sins.

He would listen, talk to us for a few moments, ask us if we were sorry for our sins, and then give us absolution for our sins and a penance that usually consisted of a few prayers, "Hail Marys," "Our Fathers," stuff like that, which we were to say in church immediately after leaving the confessional.

"Of course," said the nun, "you aren't really telling the priest your sins. When the priest is in the confessional, he is acting only as God's ears. A priest can never repeat anything he's heard in the confessional. Many priests throughout history have chosen to die rather than violate the secrecy of the confessional."

I imagined Father O'Reilly standing in front of some nebulous king, choosing to die rather than tell the king I had disobeyed my parents twice the previous week.

Sister told us that she knew people who had never committed even one mortal sin in their entire lives. If we ever did, she said, we'd never forget the first time. Sister said that if she ever committed a mortal sin, she'd be afraid to cross the street for fear someone would run her over and she'd go straight to Hell.

"Believe it or not," she said, "sisters can be sent to Hell. I would even suspect," said our nun, who was now almost whispering, "that somewhere in Hell there may be a priest." The last four words sped out of her mouth lest the crucifix on the wall overhear.

No, we didn't believe it. And no, we didn't believe that either.

After school, a group of us guys were playing softball in the vacant lot next door to Depki's house. The Depki family owned half the lot. They hadn't drunk that up yet. No one knew who owned the other half of the lot. Not much softball actually got played in Depki's field because of the sour apple tree in the middle of the field. There were about a million rules covering what happened when the softball went into the tree so we spent most of our time arguing about what branch the ball hit. Usually we played softball on the street but the neighborhood police were on another crime-prevention kick and were chasing us off before we could even get the game started.

Depki was both happy and angry about all the Confession news. He was happy because he had been told by Father O'Reilly that he now had a clean slate when he had already presumed it had been pretty well banged up.

"All this time," Depki said, "my old lady's been telling me about how I'm gonna hafta spend a lot of time in Hell for being such a jerk and here all the time I hadn't even reached the age of reason yet. Didn't even know I was doing wrong. What a fantastic deal. I just wish they had told me about this age of reason stuff sooner so I could have made more of it. Now, it's too late."

Johnny Hellger was there that day, too. Johnny was the number-one man on that infamous list of guys

I wasn't supposed to hang around with. He was always causing trouble but he rarely got caught in it himself. I guess it was because he was a very calculating type of guy. When Johnny Hellger reached into a box of candy for a chocolate cream, he got a chocolate cream.

Hellger said that he was going to commit a mortal sin the first chance he got. He figured that, sooner or later, he was going to anyway so he might as well get the first one out of the way.

I myself was overawed with this new power of being able to do something as horrendous as a mortal sin. Not that I'd ever commit one. Never. But just having the power within me to condemn myself to Hell. It was very impressive in a lousy sort of way.

Tom Lanner, who was a tall, blond-haired, easygoing friend of mine, kind of agreed with everyone. He always did. Not that he was terribly wishy-washy or anything like that. He was just very agreeable. That's all.

I felt kind of sorry for Lanner. He lived with his mother and sister in one of the few buildings in the neighborhood that could qualify as a bona fide shack. His father was dead, I guess.

Like Depki, Lanner wished he had learned about "the age of reason" earlier. Like myself, he was overawed with this new-found power of self-condemnation. And in a way, Lanner thought the same as Johnny Hellger. Lanner also felt that he would probably commit a mortal sin fairly soon. Not that Lanner wanted to commit one. He just figured that, with his lousy luck, he'd inevitably fall into one.

For the next few weeks, our nun conducted mock confessions during Catechism class. She would call on someone and he would stand up and say, "Bless me father for I have sinned. It has been one week since my last confession. I lied six times, disobeyed my parents three times, and didn't do my homework once."

As part of the mock confession, our nun would ask the kid if he was sorry for his sins just as the priest would do in the real thing. In the spirit of the mock, the kid would reply that he was and she'd give him a mock absolution for his sins and a mock penance of three "Our Fathers" and three "Hail Marys." The only kid who goofed up the dry runs was Richard Dumple, who actually told his sins, with explicit detail, in front of the room's eighty-four other kids.

The nun had us say "one week since my last confession" in the dry runs so we'd get into the habit of telling the priest how long it had been since our last confession even though we were supposed to say "this is my first confession" the first time we went.

On Friday afternoon, our nun told us to start keeping track of our sins because the following Thursday we were going to go to Confession for the first time. The Sunday after that, we would make our First Holy Communion.

First Confession and First Holy Communion were usually made a few days apart. Although Confession required a lot more training, First Holy Communion was considered the more important of the two sacraments. In Confession, our souls were cleansed of our sins. But in Holy Communion we received the actual body and blood of Christ.

Making First Holy Communion was one of the three high points in one's life, the other two being the sacrament of Confirmation, which came somewhere around fifth grade, the exact time being dependent on when the bishop could get to the parish, and Graduation Day, which, logically enough, came at the end of eighth grade.

Each of these occasions was commemorated at home by a Saturday of cleaning the basement, returning empty pop bottles, getting more ice from the store and more folding chairs from the neighbors. Then a Sunday of open house, three-dollar envelopes from relatives, a one-inch-high, one-yard-square white frosting cherry vanilla cake with CONGRATULATIONS TO . . . fill in the appropriate name . . . ON THIS MOST HOLY AND HAPPY DAY scribbled on top in red icing. And wondering on Monday morning which uncle left all the half-drunk beer cans in the dining room.

On First Holy Communion Sunday, the girls wore white lace dresses and veils, white socks, and white patent leather shoes. The girls got to keep their outfits. The boys dressed in white suits too, but rented their outfits from Silverstein Formal Wear, whose advertisement could be found in the highest box on the left side of the stage curtain in the school basement. For such major social functions, girls always kept, boys always rented.

On Thursday morning, my First Confession Day, my class solemnly and silently filed into the basement church and formed lines at the different confessionals, girls on the left side of the confessionals, boys on the right side.

St. Bastion Parish actually had two churches in one building. The upstairs church was for the adults while the church in the basement was for the kids.

Standing ten kids back in line, I was slowly being towed toward the confessional door as it continually opened and closed, sucking in one kid as it spat out another. Now I was at the front of the line, waiting for the kid in the confessional to tell his sins so I could take his place in the conscience cleaner.

Fortunately, at that time, my sins fell into two major categories: disobeying my parents and lying. During the past week I had meticulously recorded each of my sins, under the proper heading, in a brown memo notebook. Through careful tabulations on my way to school that morning, I had determined that I had disobeyed my parents three times and had lied five times during the previous week. I assigned the responsibility of remembering how many times I disobeyed my parents to my left hand, which hung innocently at my side with three fingers open. My right hand, assigned to keep track of lies, hung at my side with all five fingers open. I considered myself extremely fortunate that for this first time, when the least little forgotten detail could screw up the whole thing, my sins had not outnumbered my fingers.

As I mentally reviewed the classroom mock confessions in my mind, I could hear Depki, who was standing in line behind me, mumbling to himself. Man, he was talking double figures. Even Johnny Hellger, who was right behind Depki, wasn't goofing around as much as he usually was. At least I couldn't hear him.

The confessional door eased open in front of me. One of my classmates came out, gave me a guilty look, and slipped into one of the pews to say his penance. I stepped into the black cubicle, quickly pulling the door closed behind me.

Kneeling in front of the window, I felt my knee caps rising and falling among the pitted crevices of the kneelers. A crucifix hung over the window. It was just He and me. My mind started rattling off a lot of silent "Our Fathers" and "Hail Marys" while constantly interspersing between them, "Left-hand fingers, disobeying my parents, right-hand fingers, lying." Mumblings came from the other side of the window. The confession of the kid from the other side. I silently started praying faster to get my mind off the mumblings. We had been warned that we'd burn plenty for listening to someone else's confession.

The mumbling stopped. I heard the wooden panel slide back from my window. This was it.

"Bless me father for I have sinned. It's been one week since my last confession."

The voice behind the screen said, "I thought this was your first confession." I recognized the voice as that of the young, newly ordained priest who had just recently been assigned to St. Bastion Parish, Father Krowley.

"That's right, Father. Bless me father for I have sinned. It's been one week . . . this is my first confession. I . . ." left hand, three fingers . . . "lied three times . . ." count the fingers on the right hand . . . "disobeyed my parents five times."

The voice behind the screen started giving me a pep talk.

"You realize, of course, that when you lie to others you are really telling them that you have little faith in yourself as a human being and you have little faith in your God. Further, you should always try to obey your parents for they have devoted their lives to raising you in the image and likeness of God."

He went on and on. First Confession and I had to have the luck of drawing a dedicated priest. I could feel my knee caps beginning to crack from the pressure of the kneeler. I kept replying, "Yes Father, yes Father, yes Father," hoping he'd stop. But the words kept right on coming.

What were those kids who were waiting in line outside the door thinking? Hellger's probably mumbling to Depki, "Christ, that Ryan must have done some beauts. He's been in there a couple of hours already."

And still the priest talked. "Yes Father, yes Father, yes Father. A . . . Father, I have to go to the bathroom." I really did, too.

"Oh, yes, why of course, son. Are you sorry for your sins?"

"Yes, Father."

"For your penance then, say two 'Our Fathers' and two 'Hail Marys.' Now go in peace and God bless you."

As I stepped out of the confessional door, I heard Hellger whisper at me from behind Depki. "Hey, Ryan, who did you murder?" After I finished saying my penance, it was lunchtime and since only half of the class had gone to Confession, we were told to go home for lunch and meet back in the church basement at one o'clock.

On the way home, Johnny Hellger was still giving it to me about spending so much time in the confessional. He was trying to get Depki to razz me too, but Depki's mind seemed to be on other things. Johnny Hellger wasn't bothering me. I was too busy going over in my mind the details of that First Confession.

Things had gone surprisingly well. The only minor slipup had been the pep talk by the priest and that could hardly have been my fault. I had performed admirably. I had committed a proper variety of sins, just about the same kind that our nun had used in the dry runs. About the right number, too. Not so few that it would have seemed I had added wrong nor so many that I couldn't keep track of them with my fingers. I had handled myself well as a sinner.

At that time, when I was seven, there were two women whom I very much liked. I dreamed of them often. Whoever was starring in a particular dream would find me late at night, alone on the street. An orphan, lost, bewildered, sad-faced. She would pick me up, hug me tightly, and then take me home with her where she would rock me to sleep in her arms after having fed me milk and Campbell's Chicken Noodle Soup. Those two women were Dinah Shore and the Blessed Virgin Mary.

I had developed an intense liking for Dinah Shore through watching her fifteen-minute television program, which was on every Tuesday and Thursday night. At St. Bastion's, we were constantly told that the Blessed Virgin Mary was the second most important person in the world, second only to her son, Jesus Christ. There were a lot of statues and pictures of the Blessed Virgin Mary around St. Bastion school, which showed how pretty she was. Of course, she was always dressed in those long gowns but you could still tell that she was a nice-looking woman.

Lunch wasn't quite ready when I got home so I decided to spend a few minutes relaxing in my little red rocker. Mom was making Campbell's Chicken Noodle Soup for lunch. The aroma of the soup drifted into my nostrils. My mind on Confession already, I naturally looked up at the ceiling and began thinking about how proud the Blessed Virgin Mary must be in Heaven after seeing the brilliant way I handled myself in my First Confession. Now she knew my love was sincere and that I was a faithful apostle of her son.

With my red-rocker world rolling so smoothly over the living room rug, I decided to relive once more in my mind my First Confession so that I could again feel the exhilaration of knowing how well I had handled myself in this first venture into the world of organized sin. My mind had instant replay long before CBS.

I pulled the brown memo notebook out of my pocket and once again went over my sin tabulations.

LIES

Friday	Lied to Dad when he asked me if I had used his hammer.
Saturday	Lied to Mom when she asked me if I had broken Linda's roller skates.
Saturday	Lied to Mom when she asked me if I had taken out the dog.

Tuesday	Lied to Depki when he asked me if I had a dime he could borrow.

Total lies for the week: three.

I knew I didn't have to count the lie I told Depki because he wasn't an adult or a member of the family. Then I again went over the list of the times I had disobeyed my parents.

DISOBEYING MY PARENTS

Friday	When Dad told me to take out the garbage *now*.
Saturday	When Mom asked me to straighten out my room.
Sunday	When Mom asked me to turn down the television.
Sunday	When Dad told me to stop crying after Mom hit me for not turning down the television.
Tuesday	When Dad told me to put away my baseball stuff in the basement.
Wednesday	When Dad told me to go out and close the garage door.

Total disobeyings for the week: five.

I added them up again just to make sure. I shouldn't have. When I did, I got six disobediences instead of five. I added the disobediences up again and I got six instead of five again. I added them up a third time and got six for the third time. Good God! I had told the priest in Confession that I had disobeyed my parents five times and here I had disobeyed six times.

I brought my little red rocker to a fast halt, slamming both feet to the floor. My tongue was running around collecting saliva, slapping it up against the roof of my mouth, and sliding it down to my throat, which was gulping spasmodically.

The Blessed Virgin Mary was looking down on me all right. Looking down and thinking what a rat I was. I went over my column of lies again to see if I had also made a mistake there. Then I realized that if I had lied in Confession about how many times I had disobeyed, that was another lie for the week, which meant that I was wrong in the lying category, too. So when I told the priest how many times I had lied during the week, I had lied again. My mind was becoming engulfed in an infinity of lies. As close as I could figure, my First Confession was off by at least one disobedience and two lies.

Neither Father O'Reilly nor my classroom nun had told us what happened to someone who lied in Confession. Probably no one had ever done it before so there wasn't even a rule to cover it.

The phone rang. My mother came in from the kitchen to answer it. I knew it had to be the priest who had heard my confession. He had just found out that I had lied in Confession and was calling my mother to tell her that I was being expelled from St. Bastion school and excommunicated from the Church . . . and the country, just for starters.

"Hello? Oh, hello, Aunt Margaret. Could I call you back? The kids are home from school for lunch right now."

Aunt Margaret, who, every time she came over to the house, told me I behaved like a bed wetter. I hated her, until that phone call. She was okay in my book now. Aunt Margaret had come through when it counted.

Campbell's Chicken Noodle Soup and milk were my favorite lunchtime combination. One is very hot and the other is very cold. If I alternated them properly, I could get my teeth to feel like they were jiggling. It was a cheap but very enjoyable thrill.

But that lunchtime, I was not concerned with cheap thrills. As I sat at the lunch table, the Blessed Virgin Mary stared down at me, intoning, "How could you? How could you? How could you?" Then, for the first and one of the few times in my life, my mind reasoned out a solution.

Lying in Confession is a sin, right? Right. And you're supposed to tell your sins in Confession, right? Right. So this afternoon, when your class meets in the basement church in order for the other half of the class to go to Confession, you go to Confession again and tell the priest about the sins you committed in your First Confession.

"That's it!"

"That's what?" asked my mother. "Is the soup too hot?"

"No, Mom. The soup's perfect." The rest of the lunch was spent in cheap thrills.

That afternoon, when we met in church, Sister said, "Those of you who have already gone to Confession, kneel in one of the pews and say some extra prayers. The rest of you who still have to go to Confession, line up at the confessional doors like the other children did this morning."

Nobody noticed I was in the confessional line for the second time until Johnny Hellger turned around in his pew and saw me. He was really impressed. Johnny Hellger had always more or less taken me for a chump. Now it was apparent that I was so rotten I had to go to Confession twice a day.

"For Christ's sake, Ryan," Johnny Hellger whispered, "what do you do during lunchtime?"

In the black cubicle, listening for the sliding wooden panel.

"Bless me father for I have sinned. It has been one hour and ten minutes since my last confession."

Twenty seconds later I was free from sin, free from sin, free from sin. When I went to sleep that night, the Blessed Virgin Mary once more found me alone on the street. An orphan. Lost, bewildered, sad-faced. She picked me up, hugged me tightly, and took me home with her where she rocked me to sleep in her arms after having fed me milk and Campbell's Chicken Noodle Soup. Never again did I dream of Dinah Shore.

Confession gradually became as much a routine in my life as mass on Sunday and no meat on Fridays. The categories of sin increased as did the number of sins in the categories. The holes in my soul or the nails of Venial Sin that caused them no longer gnawed at my conscience with the same vitality that they had only a couple of years earlier. The increase was gradual so I didn't notice it that much. Committing more sins seemed to be another inevitable cost of growing up, like getting more homework. Besides, venial sins were insignificant. No matter how many I committed, they couldn't send me to Hell. Mortal Sin was where the action was.

In third and fourth grade, I spent most of my time hanging around with Johnny Hellger, who by then had become THE kid in the neighborhood to hang around with. Hellger's popularity was based on the fact that his life-style closely resembled that of the neighborhood's hero. Bugs Bunny.

The easiest way to find out what heroes are popular in a particular neighborhood is to check out the lunch boxes. But the lunch boxes carried by the kids of St. Bastion Parish weren't smothered with the faces of Gene Autry, Roy Rogers, the Blue Fairy, or any of the other big names. Most of our lunch boxes were colored gunmetal gray with nothing but "Made in U.S.A. by Union Workers" stamped on the bottom of them. Bugs Bunny didn't pedal lunch boxes. He was above all that.

Johnny Hellger, like every other kid in Seven Holy Tombs, was a punk. But unlike most of us run-of-the-mill punks, Johnny Hellger actually won. He would steal and not get caught. He'd lie and no one would care. He would disobey and everyone would forget. Johnny Hellger was indeed a proficient protégé of Bugs Bunny, that most professional of punks.

Today, Bugs Bunny would be called an antiestablishment figure. Then, he was just a punk. But unlike us punks in the St. Bastion world of everyday reality, Bugs Bunny always won. He'd sucker Elmer Fudd into catastrophes almost at will and not once did Bugs ever lose a round to Yosemite Sam.

Bugs Bunny was a punk's punk. But since he didn't live in the neighborhood, the kids of Seven Holy Tombs sought out the next best thing, the company of Johnny Hellger. I was one of the few chosen from the many.

Johnny Hellger and I did all sorts of rotten things together. We climbed people's garages, cut across their yards, stomped through their bushes, rang their doorbells and ran, played in construction areas, pitched pennies on the sidewalk, and went over to Seven Holy Tombs Public School and yelled "sucker" outside the school's windows on days that St. Bastion's had off and the public schools didn't.

Johnny Hellger also used to steal candy bars from the grocery stores. I never did any of that, though. Climbing people's garages seemed fair. Stealing candy bars didn't. Besides, I was too chicken.

I did swipe some Baker's chocolate from my mother's cabinet once, but that didn't work out too well.

Pure Baker's chocolate tastes something like brown sand.

Like most bad habits, it took a lot of money to keep up with Johnny Hellger. On my twenty-five-cent-a-week allowance, it simply couldn't be done, legitimately. So I began pilfering nickels and dimes from around the house. After a while I moved up to quarters and on occasion even snatched half-dollars.

I wasn't in danger of committing Mortal Sin, though. I had checked it out right at the beginning of the school year with my nun during a Catechism class.

The four questions we had had to memorize for that morning's lesson were on Mortal Sin. I raised my hand and, in an extremely objective tone of voice so as not to cast any shadow of suspicion on myself, asked Sister a question.

"Str, how much money would someone have to steal in order for it to be a mortal sin?"

"Oh, it would have to be quite a lot of money," she said. Generalities wouldn't do. I needed specifics.

"How much, Str?"

"A dollar, I'd say."

She had taken the vow of poverty, all right. But it seemed a logical enough line of division to me. Change couldn't have been too big a thing. I handled it all the time myself: going to the store, buying school supplies, getting stuff at the dime store. I rarely got to touch paper money. A dollar sounded just about right for a mortal sin.

A few days after I found out what it cost to commit a mortal sin, Johnny Hellger asked me to go to Woolworth's with him to buy some French fries. I was tempted to steal four quarters from the house to finance the venture, but I didn't. It wouldn't have really been a mortal since since it wasn't actually a dollar. But I knew four quarters would more likely be

41

missed by one of my parents than even a dollar so I didn't take them.

On Sunday morning, Johnny Hellger called me up and asked me if I wanted to go to the show with him that afternoon. The show was quite a distance from Seven Holy Tombs, a thirty-minute bus ride and you had to transfer buses twice. At that time I was allowed to go only with my older sister and then only rarely. For one thing, such an expedition took a tremendous amount of money. At least a dollar seventy-five.

I scrounged around my bedroom and could come up with only eighty cents. On the way to the breakfast table I saw it, a crumpled-up dollar underneath the dining room table centerpiece, an orange fruit bowl devoid of fruit.

I knew Johnny Hellger would be unmerciful in his derision of me if I failed to go to the show with him. He'd presume that the reason I wouldn't go was that I was afraid to disobey my parents and leave the neighborhood without my sister. Hardly an acceptable excuse.

I decided to have breakfast first. Maybe the dollar would be gone when I finished. It wasn't. Standing in the dining room and staring at the crumpled-up dollar bill for minutes. What the heck, there was no rush. I didn't have to tell Hellger whether I was going to the show or not until one o'clock.

I went outside and played baseball for a few hours, hoping the dollar bill would disappear by the time I got back to the house.

Saying silent prayers as I hurried through the dining room with my baseball equipment. A momentary weakness. A glance. It was still there. Stopping. Many times in the past few months I had almost stolen a dollar. Somehow, I knew this time would be more than a temptation. I recalled the words of my nun, who had told of the deadliness of Mortal Sin.

"If you commit a mortal sin, you are spiritually dead in the eyes of God. And if you die with it on your soul before you get a chance to tell it in Confession, you go straight to Hell. The only thing that can save you between the time you commit the mortal sin and the time you go to Confession is saying a perfect act of contrition to God. But a perfect act of contrition is actually a perfect prayer of love to God. Very few people are holy enough to make a perfect act of contrition. And since those people love God so much, they never commit mortal sins anyway. Yes, children, I'm afraid that perfect acts of contrition are very hard to come by."

I thought of that bald, bulgy-faced cowboy who always played the leader of the bad guys on television. I saw him handing a gun to one of his cronies, who always called him boss, and saying to him, "Don't worry, Louie, your first murder's always the toughest." It was the same for Mortal Sin.

Who am I kidding? I said to myself. Last Wednesday I almost decided to steal a dollar. The week before that I almost did, too. If I don't steal a dollar today, I'll probably steal one tomorrow or the next day so I might as well steal it when I need it.

But my conscience wouldn't quit. It kept yelling, "Damned for eternity. Spiritually dead." I knew that if I kept listening to my conscience, I'd be out a dollar. I had to act fast. Grabbed. The act was committed. I was in the state of Mortal Sin.

My first compulsion was to spend it. I was afraid I'd put the dollar back and then not only would I be in the state of Mortal Sin but I'd also be out the dollar as well.

I raced outside, hopped on my bike, and went to four neighborhood grocery stores and bought a quarter's worth of candy at each. I couldn't buy a dollar's worth at any one of them. Such a large purchase would have aroused suspicions in the owner, which would have been reported back to my parents.

The autumn afternoon was already dying when I began home, walking my bike down the cinder alley that ran along the back of my block and behind my house. Half of the candy was souring in my stomach, the remainder of it lay in a brown paper bag clenched in my fist. As I shoved the bike wheels through the loose cinders, I flipped the bag into a neighbor's uncovered garbage can.

Already spiritual rigor mortis was beginning to set in. Spiritually dead. I couldn't even go to Holy Communion because one of the rules stated that if a person had a mortal sin on his soul, he couldn't receive any of the other sacraments or he'd be committing another mortal sin.

Damned for eternity. If I died between now and the time I went to Confession, I would go to Hell for a dollar.

I suddenly realized that I had indeed picked a bad time to commit a mortal sin: Sunday afternoon. St. Bastion Church didn't hold any confessions until the following Saturday afternoon. I was eternally damned for at least a week.

I was dying by the time I got home. The consumed candy, which I thought had gone to my stomach, had instead coagulated in the middle of my throat, refusing to budge.

"Johnny Hellger called you this afternoon while you were out," my mother said. "He mentioned something about you going to the show. You weren't planning on going to the show with him, were you?"

"Of course not." I choked out the words around the glop of goo in my throat. "Even if I was allowed to go that far by myself, I don't have any money."

"I told him he must be mistaken," my mother said. "You know your father and I don't like you hanging around with that boy. Why, his own mother doesn't even know where he is half of the time."

I was going to say, "Neither does Hellger," but that would have just prolonged the conversation and I didn't feel much like talking.

It wasn't until the next morning that I decided God had allowed that dollar to be placed in my path as a test because He was planning on having me die that week and wanted to see if I deserved to go to Heaven or Hell. His conclusions were all too apparent to me. I convinced myself that perhaps if I was real careful and didn't expose myself to any unnecessary dangers, God would let me live another week until I had time to go to Confession on Saturday afternoon.

I faked being sick on Monday so I could stay in the safety of my house. During the rest of the week, when I walked to and from school, I constantly watched for cars to swerve out of control to try and run me over on the sidewalk. I didn't play outside. My mother had told me once about a kid who had died while playing outside. At night, I stayed awake as long as possible. If I was going to die, I wanted to be around when it happened. Saturday took years to come.

Confessions at St. Bastion's were held from three to five o'clock on Saturday afternoons. I got to the church around two-thirty and waited around outside in front of the building until about three-thirty. I wanted to give the priests a chance to get into their confessionals so they wouldn't see me when I came in.

As soon as I got into church, I knelt down in the last pew and pretended to pray. Actually, I was trying to figure out which of the six confessionals was the safest to enter. In those days, there were no names on the outside of the confessionals identifying the priest who was inside. You had to gamble if you wanted your sins forgiven.

There were two priests I could not afford to get: Father O'Reilly and Father Luvan.

Whenever I had gone to Confession to Father O'Reilly, he had always seemed reluctant to forgive me for my sins. And those were only venial sins. I was afraid he might not even forgive a mortal sin even though I knew he was supposed to.

Father Luvan was a very nice priest but he was deaf. Anyone who went to Father Luvan for Confession had to shout their sins all over the church.

The ideal priest to get would have been Father Lupienski, a Hungarian priest who had been in this country for only a few months. Father Lupienski was a very friendly guy who smiled and said hello to everyone he met, although he never stopped to talk to any of the parishioners.

Depki told me that he had gone to Confession four weeks in a row to Father Lupienski and no matter what sins Depki told him, Father Lupienski always gave him the same penance, three "Our Fathers" and three "Hail Marys."

Depki suspected. The next time Depki got Father Lupienski in Confession, he told him that he had lied thirty-eight thousand times to his parents.

"Are you sorry for your sins?" aasked Father Lupienski.

"Yes, Father," said Depki.

"Then for your penance, say three 'Our Fathers' and three 'Hail Marys.'"

It was apparent, said Depki, that although Father Lupienski had memorized a few lines of it, he neither spoke nor understood any English.

For an hour I knelt in the last pew of St. Bastion Church, trying to tell by the length of the lines who was controlling what confessionals. It didn't take a line to tell me what confessional Father Luvan was in.

46

I could hear him shouting all over the church. "Tell me your sins again and louder please, I can't hear you." There was no line at all forming at confessional number three. The word had passed. Father O'Reilly was lurking there.

As long as I knew where those two were, I was okay. It really didn't matter that much who I got as long as the priest was halfway human. I was hoping I'd get Father Lupienski but it wasn't absolutely necessary.

I got in line over at confessional number five. I wasn't worried about dying anymore; even if God grabbed me right there I was sure he'd give me some credit for at least being in church. The line moved along quickly. In a few moments I was kneeling down in the confessional.

While I waited for the priest to come to my side of the confessional, I practiced whispering in a phony voice so he wouldn't be able to recognize me if he ever heard me outside the confessional. Not that I was worried he'd tell anyone about my mortal sin. I just didn't like the idea of him knowing who did it.

Hearing the wooden panel slide back from my confessional window, I waited for the priest to ask me to begin because then I'd know who he was. I knew the voices of all the St. Bastion priests.

"Yes," he said, "please begin." It was the voice of Father Durlin, the young assistant priest.

"Bless me father for I have sinned. It has been one week since my last confession. I have committed the mortal sin of stealing." I had forgotten to use my phony voice. It was too late now.

"What did you steal?"

"I stole a dollar."

"That's not a mortal sin."

"It's not?"

"No, it's not. Who told you stealing a dollar is a mortal sin?"

"The sister in school."

"Well, she's wrong."

"She's wrong?"

"She's wrong. Stealing a dollar is not enough to constitute a mortal sin. Did you commit any other sins this past week?"

"Uh, yes, Father, but I can't remember them right now."

"No other mortal sins?"

"Oh no, Father, no other mortal sins."

"Fine. When you remember your other sins, tell them in your next confession. Now for your penance, I want you to say a decade of the rosary and while you're saying it I want you to think about Christ and how He suffered and died on the cross for your sins. Now go in peace and God bless you."

I burst out of the confessional door, slid into an empty pew, and said two quick decades of the rosary, the extra one for God allowing me to live long enough to get to Confession. Then a quick genuflection, a two-finger dip in the holy water as I shot by the door, and I was out.

What a fantastic feeling! To come back from the spiritually dead. To be free from sin! free from sin! free from sin! As I walked through the neighborhood, brown igloos of raked leaves smoldered lazily, scenting the air with their familiar fall fragrance. The world fit so comfortably around me that everything I saw and heard seemed as if it had just been given, as I had, a brand new shot at life. Even Billy Schmidt, a kid with whom I shared a mutual hate, looked good to me as I passed him on the street. I said hello to him and he was so shocked that he said hello back. When I got home, my favorite dinner, fried chicken, was already on the table. The Jackie Gleason show was on at 6:30 and Mom even said we could eat on trays in the living room.

I can remember my most amusing confession. I was in college and I had stopped in a small-town church on my way into Chicago one Friday afternoon. A nun had a class of children going to Confession. I simply got in line with them.

In the confessional, I recited my sins. After I finished, there was a long pause followed by an old, tired voice.

"Those are some sins for a fifth grader."

And I remember the last one. Kneeling in a confessional in some city's cathedral. When the priest asked me if I was sorry for my sins, in a moment of indifference, I gave him an honest answer. He shouted. I left. By then, there was more than a darkened window separating us.

Down the steps of the cathedral knowing, no, hoping in my mind that I was right yet realizing I was never again to feel that resurgence of faith in my own and the world's immortality. Never again to experience the exhilaration of rising from the spiritually dead. Never again to be free from sin, free from sin, free from sin.

IV *Father O'Reilly*

Father O'Reilly, pastor of St. Bastion Parish, was a priest who took a totally Old Testament attitude toward the souls God had entrusted to him. He was strictly a company man. Either you played according to the rules of the Catholic Church or he told you to go to Hell. He was our shepherd and we were his sheep. And if a sheep got out of line, Father O'Reilly cut his head off.

He was the one-man Mafia of Seven Holy Tombs. Father O'Reilly controlled the entire neighborhood, everyone and everything in it, with simple brute force. He was worse than the Mafia for he had God on his side.

If a Catholic kid was picked up by the police in Seven Holy Tombs, he was given the choice of being taken to either the police station or to St. Bastion's Rectory and Father O'Reilly. Most made the wise choice of the police station.

Like many men of power, Fatther O'Reilly was a financial wizard. He had come to Seven Holy Tombs and founded St. Bastion Parish in the early 1920s, when the parish was little more than a few scattered farms. The first parish church was a deserted barn. By the late 1920s, when the depression struck, the town of Seven Holy Tombs numbered a few thousand.

During those depression years, Father O'Reilly kept the parish going by selling chickens door to door. No one knew where the chickens came from. They were Round Neck chickens, a breed of chicken rarely found in this country. Some of the early parishioners who survived the depression with him claimed that if it hadn't been for Father O'Reilly and his Round Neck chickens, they would have lost their homes.

It was also during the depression that Father O'Reilly began his greatest commercial coup, the legendary St. Bastion Carnival. Although its beginnings were probably humble, by the early 1950s it had mushroomed into a fantastic financial four-day kill.

As is true of most monetary geniuses, Father O'Reilly diversified his financial interests. There was the annual chancebook crusade, two cents a chance, a dollar for a book. A member of the clergy almost always won the grand-prize Ford Thunderbird. There were pantry showers for the nuns, bake sales, mission money drives, and of course the traditional Sunday mass pass-the-basket collections. But the biggest event was the yearly St. Bastion Carnival.

One day, at the beginning of the school year, we kids would look out the school windows and see five or six wooden braces standing on the playground. They had been set up the night before by some men of the parish. The braces would have multiplied themselves by the time we came back to school the next day. By Thursday, the entire school yard would be a field of beam stalks. On Thursday night, we'd go back to the playground and, while whispering speculations to one another about the wooden crates of prizes and carnival counters that were being carted in, watch the parish men roll the green canvas across the braces.

There were at least forty or fifty booths under the green canvas. There were dart booths, ringlet booths, ball-and-metal-milk-bottle booths, guess-your-weight-within-five-pounds booths, and just plain reach-in-the-jar-and-try-and-pull-out-a-winning-number booths.

In the center of the playground was the major attraction—the bingo game. It was formed by about two dozen metal-top folding tables arranged in a large square, marking the boundaries of the game. Each table was armed with a number of ashtrays filled with corn kernels, the ashtrays courtesy of "Smiling Sam, he's a Gas, Service Station."

In the middle of the bingo square piled high on wooden racks were the prizes: blankets, five-dollar dinnerware, stuffed animals, religious statues and ukuleles. In front of the prizes was the revolving wire barrel that spat out an appropriately marked poker chip on every third hand-turned revolution.

"Are you ready, ladies and gentlemen?" Father O'Reilly's voice would wrinkle through the static-filled public-address system. Parish men hustled by the bingo tables, their coin-crammed hardware-store aprons looped under their navels, snatching dimes and quarters from fingers while simultaneously retrieving old bingo cards that had failed to win and dispensing new hopefuls.

Players' hands scooped up kernals of corn from "Smiling Sam, he's a Gas, Service Station" ashtrays and wrapped the kernels into fists. The corn kernels were allowed to drip out until the weight of the fists was just right. Then one kernel would pry itself loose from the others and work its way up until it nudged itself comfortably between the thumb and index finger. The fist would slowly settle onto the bingo card. Ready.

"I 17," Father O'Reilly's voice would bellow through the canvas-covered playground. The first four numbers were swiftly called. It takes five to win in bingo. But beginning with the fifth call, Father O'Reilly's words ventured out cautiously.

"G 28," he'd rasp into the microphone. If the next few seconds passed unmolested, a united sigh of relief would shiver through the silence. Father O'Reilly would whisper the next number, "O 17." Inevitably a voice would tear through the tension, hysterically screaming BINGO. Around the bingo tables some of the Ten Commandments would fall to the mumblings of the losers.

Bingo could have been fun if it hadn't been for Mrs. Murphy. Like all old ladies, Mrs. Murphy had natural bingo ability. But even taking into consideration Mrs. Murphy's advantage of being an old lady, she was exceptionally good, winning almost every game she played. People came away from the bingo tables repeating the word "bingo" to themselves just to see if their lips could really form the word.

Mrs. Murphy died a few years ago. It would be nice to report that she had a nephew with a sense of humor who had Mrs. Murphy's tombstone inscribed solely with her favorite word. That's the way it should have been, but it wasn't.

Among us kids, the most popular booth was the goldfish-bowl booth. A regulation goldfish-bowl booth consisted of a wooden railing, a table twelve feet beyond covered with small round goldfish bowls, two goldfish to a bowl, and lots of Ping-Pong balls.

It cost ten cents to toss three Ping-Pong balls at the table, no reaching over the railing. If you landed a Ping-Pong ball into a goldfish bowl, you won.

Rare was the kid in my parish who went through eight years of grammar school without winning a goldfish bowl. Rarer still was a goldfish from my parish who lived longer than a week.

I was in third grade when I won my goldfish bowl. I had spent the better part of the previous three days practicing in the bathroom by standing in a corner of the tub, in order to bet the proper distance, and pitching wads of paper into the toilet.

Upon arriving at the carnival that Sunday afternoon, it took me four Ping-Pong balls to discover that toilets and goldfish bowls don't have a lot in common. The fifth Ping-Pong ball hit a rim of one of the goldfish bowls. But instead of ricocheting off the table as most Ping-Pong balls would have done, it went straight up and came down in a goldfish bowl. I was delirious. It was the first time in my life I had gotten something in life that I had wanted and didn't deserve to get. I named my two goldfish Bill and Fred.

When I got Bill and Fred home, I was shocked at my parents' indifferent attitude toward my victorious return. Here I had left only three hours earlier with nothing but sixty-five cents in my pocket and a little hope that I might somehow break even with Father O'Reilly's carnival. Now I had scored big and still had fifteen cents left. I hadn't won a lousy stuffed animal or some plastic toy donated by Woolworth's, I had won two goldfish and a bowl. I went to put Bill and Fred on top of the television.

"Don't put them there," my father said, "they'll interfere with the reception."

"Okay, I'll put them on the kitchen counter. That way they'll be close to fresh running water."

"Fine, fine," he said and went back to reading his newspaper.

While I was getting Bill and Fred situated on the kitchen counter, my mother was rinsing off potatoes in the sink for supper.

"I'm going to have to go out and buy Bill and Fred a big tank tomorrow and some goldfish food too," I said. "And then I'll teach them a lot of tricks."

"You don't have to buy them food," my mother said. "They can eat small pieces of bread. And you can't teach them any tricks. Goldfish don't do tricks."

"What do you mean goldfish don't do tricks?"

"I mean," she was putting weight behind her words now, "that goldfish don't do tricks. They just swim around."

"That's not much," I said.

"It is if you're a goldfish."

By Tuesday, Bill was swimming on his side and Fred was beginning to do the same thing. I thought maybe the Ping-Pong balls had managed to plunk both of them in the head so instead of just serving them pieces of bread, I put butter on the bread first. Bill and Fred looked like they could use the extra nourishment.

When I got home from school on Thursday, the goldfish bowl was on the counter, empty and smelly.

"Where are my goldfish?"

"I flushed them down the toilet," my mother said.

"Why did you do that?"

"Because they were dead."

That came as no shock to me. On the way home from school, Depki had warmed me about the usual life expectancy of a carnival-won goldfish. But flushing them down the toilet?

54

"Why didn't you bury them?" I asked. "I thought Catholics buried things when they died." When mad, go after a person's jugular vein, their religion.

"We do, but not goldfish. The goldfish weren't Catholic."

"How do you know? They came from a Catholic carnival, didn't they?"

My mother turned around and gave me a look that said the conversation was over.

I went upstairs and peered into the toilet. Nothing. Bill and Fred were now forever in that world where all things dropped into the toilet go.

I went over to Depki's house and told him about my goldfish. He wasn't surprised. "That's the same thing my old lady did, except she flushed them down the toilet the next day. I don't even think they were dead. You know what they oughta do at that carnival."

"What's that?"

"They oughta give away dogs. You can't flush a dog down a toilet."

While the carnival was being held on the playground, a spaghetti dinner was being served in the school basement. Six rows of tables ran across the entire length of the basement from the entrance doors right up to the base of the stage.

A whisper could be whipped into locomotive strength by the acoustics of the school basement. The noise of a St. Bastion Carnival dinner crowd would assault the walls with such intensity that sound would be sucked dry before it could travel even a few feet. Everyone talked but no one heard.

The spaghetti dinner without meatballs was a dollar. You could eat as much as you liked but you normally learned your lesson after the first plateful. Dessert was from the tray of donated delicacies at the end of the table.

On the following Monday, all the leftover spaghetti

became macaroni and was served to the school children at ten cents a plate. The next day, approximately 20 percent of the school population would contract the twenty-four-hour crippler commonly known as Carnival Cramps.

As an added enticement to attending the carnival, the name of a different parishioner would be announced over the public-address system every hour. If the parishioner reported to the bingo booth in the following five minutes, he got five dollars. If he wasn't around, another name was announced. Father O'Reilly didn't believe in living room winners.

Father O'Reilly's carnival would begin in the early evening hours of Friday night and rage right through the weekend until the early hours of Monday morning snuffed it out. For those three days, St. Bastion Parish whirled around like an unknotted balloon. But by Monday morning, the air had passed. The balloon was flat.

As we'd pass the school playground on the way to our classrooms, we'd see the green canvas lying exhausted across the braces, waiting for the men of the parish to get home from work so they could come and take her down. All the prizes would be gone from beneath her, even the metal milk bottles would already have been packed away for another year. All that would remain would be the hollow booths surrounded by scattered ticket stubs discarded by sweaty hands that had hoped in vain for a winner. What a miserable day to be alive. But the postcarnival Monday morning of fourth grade was the most miserable of them all.

Depki and I used to meet at seven-thirty in the morning on the corner and walk to school together. The first thing he said that Monday morning was, "Hey, Ryan, what are you going to do with that five dollars you won?"

"What five dollars?"

"The five dollars you won at the carnival yesterday. You mean you weren't there when your name was called?"

"My name wasn't called, Depki. Who're you kidding."

He insisted it was. When we met Johnny Hellger on the way to school, I went through the same routine with him. I figured that Depki and Hellger had got together the day before and had set me up for it.

I was getting worried when Tom Lanner asked me the same thing as I was hanging up my jacket in the coatroom. By morning prayers, it was a confirmed catastrophe. I had blown five dollars by being in the wrong place at the wrong time.

The nun spent twenty minutes in front of the class asking me how I felt and what I would have done with all of that money if I had won it. Those nuns were beautiful. When you were down, could they kick.

Father O'Reilly could always be found at a St. Bastion Carnival just as he could be found at any church function, whether it was midnight mass or a janitors' meeting. He'd stand there in his seamy, shiny black cassock, his hands clasped behind his back, his eyes peering out beyond the precipice of his stomach. His whole frame would gently rise and fall as his feet rocked from heel to toe.

Father O'Reilly would spend his time talking to a few parishionners or standing in the background. He never acted as if he was running things even though everyone knew that he was. Father O'Reilly was happy to limit his performances to twice a week: Friday night novena and the Sunday morning eight o'clock mass.

Besides being Seven Holy Tombs's one-man Mafia, Father O'Reilly was also its one-man Inquisition. The

Friday night novena often served as a launching pad for one of his neighborhood raids.

He'd come out on the altar after the service and his words would growl out over the gravel in his voice to that multitude of old ladies, simple-minded men, and young married couples who thought the Friday night novena was a "night out."

"There are," Father O'Reilly would wait for his first words to engulf the church, "dirty books in Delvin's Drugstore." Father O'Reilly would wave his arm in the general direction of Delvin Drugs even though everyone in the church knew where Delvin Drugs was since it was the only drugstore in the neighborhood.

"We are not going to allow our children to be exposed to that kind of trash. We are not going to allow Delvin's Drugstore to make money on dirty books."

Then Father O'Reilly would march down 138th Street with the Friday night novena crowd right behind him and into Delvin's Drugstore where he would tell Mr. Delvin to get the dirty books off the shelves.

Since the neighborhood was mostly Catholic, Father O'Reilly could have used financial threats, but he didn't. Neither did he threaten physical violence. Father O'Reilly never hit anyone his own size. Father O'Reilly would simply tell Mr. Delvin to take the dirty books off the shelves and Mr. Delvin, like all residents of Seven Holy Tombs, would obey.

Unlike the Supreme Court, Father O'Reilly had no difficulty in determining what was a dirty book. A dirty book looked like a dirty book. You could tell a book by its cover.

Father O'Reilly never bothered to lead a raid on Dirty Shirt Andy's store even though that store was a block closer than Delvin's. It was more than rumored that Dirty Shirt Andy also had some dirty books rotting somewhere among his shelves.

Dirty Shirt Andy was simply too undependable. Father O'Reilly knew that Dirty Shirt might not be open when he got there. Sometimes you could go by Dirty Shirt Andy's store at three in the morning, look in, and see him sitting behind his Butternut Bread counter, his arms dangling over the counter, right above the "B" in the Butternut, his eyes staring past you into the darkness. Other times, the store would be closed for weeks, even though Dirty Shirt Andy lived right behind it. One of the advantages of having no business is that you don't have to worry about not being there when your customers don't show up.

Although the American Pharmaceutical Association was acutely aware of Father O'Reilly's Friday night novena raids, the average citizen of Seven Holy Tombs wasn't. The raids occurred only as the necessity arose. Father O'Reilly also realized that a lot of the old ladies couldn't stand the five-block walk to Delvin's Drugstore more than once every three months. In short, the raids were a sometime thing. But like all great geysers, Father O'Reilly had to spout off regularly and the Sunday morning eight o'clock mass was his place of burst.

Father O'Reilly, blessed with a tongue that could cut rock, believed that the best way to get people to Heaven was to scare the Hell out of them. There was plenty of weeping and gnashing of teeth when Father O'Reilly talked from the pulpit. His words rolled like a roller coaster as he sought to save your soul and have you see the light.

He'd start out slowly, calmly, nonchalantly dragging you up toward that first big dip. Even though you'd been on this ride before and knew that dip was coming, you were already getting scared. He'd work you right up to the very peak of serenity, pause a moment, and then plunge you straight down as your stomach shot up to your head. A straightaway of sheer fright and speed. Then another climb, dip, climb, dip. There wasn't a deodorant made that didn't fail a Father O'Reilly sermon.

Oddly enough, Father O'Reilly's enthusiasm encouraged a lot of people to commit Mortal Sin. He was constantly telling them to take advantage of the opportunity to go to Holy Communion at his mass as they might be dead the next day.

In order to go to Holy Communion, you had to fast from midnight and be in the "state of grace," in other words, have no unconfessed mortal sins on your soul. If you didn't fast and you weren't in the state of grace but you went ahead and received Holy Communion anyway, you committed another mortal sin.

It required a person with a lot of moxie to remain in his place while the rest of the people in his pew clumped by him to go to the Communion rail. You could always claim you had accidentally broken your fast but then, you knew what you'd be thinking if someone else had remained in his pew.

The kids' eight o'clock mass in the basement church always ended before Father O'Reilly's mass, which was going on in the upstairs church for the adults. During our mass, we would hear his thunder overhead and would wonder what it was like to be so close to lightning. After our mass, some of us would wait around in front of the church for our parents to get out. A few minutes later, we would see them teetering through the pine doors, giddy, numb, dazed, sick to their stomachs, thankful to be off the roller coaster for another seven days.

One early morning in April the nuns lined us up in front of the basement church doors and told us that since the basement church had got some rain the night before, we were going to have to stand in the back of the upstairs church and attend the adult eight o'clock mass.

What a break! It was like my mother running out of milk and asking me if I'd mind having beer with my peanut butter and jelly sandwich. Father O'Reilly's eight o'clock mass sermons were, like drinking and smoking, only for those of legal age or older. We were, in effect, being handed a visa to the adult world.

The first part of the mass was uneventful. No one came in late, of course, just as no one would try and sneak out of mass early. Such attempts were stopped by Father O'Reilly, who, upon seeing the aspiring escapee trying to crawl out of church, would yell at him from the altar. "Can't even give God an hour of your time, huh. He gives you a life and you can't even give Him an hour a week."

The altar boys stepped cautiously as they moved about the altar. Serving mass for Father O'Reilly was considered slightly more difficult than walking on water. Some of those altar boys would grow up and spend the better part of their adulthood in neighborhood taverns sopping up free drinks and reliving heroic moments of Father O'Reilly masses while a few of the faithful would gather around the barstool and shake their heads in affirmative disbelief.

When it came time for the sermon, Father O'Reilly casually walked over and leaned his huge bulk against the lectern, flopping his flabby arms on top of it. He paused a moment, making sure all eyes in the church were riveted on him, before he began. His first words came matter-of-factly, almost in a whisper, as if he were presenting a commentary on the ten o'clock news.

"Saw Ed Connery at this mass last Sunday morning. He was sitting in the third pew right over there. He was on time for mass, paid attention. Went to Holy Communion. Then he went home and had breakfast with his wife and six kids. Decided to go into the living room and watch a little television. Ed Connery turned the set on and went to sit in his easy chair. He was dead before he got there." PAUSE. THINK ABOUT THAT YOU BASTARDS. "We buried Ed on Tuesday morning.

"Ed was sitting here with us last Sunday morning, a healthy man, younger than most of you." The roller coaster words of Father O'Reilly began to CLIMB CLIMB CLIMB. "Had a beautiful family, except for the second youngest, who did poorly in school, had a good job, nice home," CLIMB, CLIMB CLIMB, "yet God decided that Ed Connery's time had come."

Like all great roller coasters, Father O'Reilly paused a moment before the big plunge. And then, THE PLUNGE. "Maybe we'll be burying You next Tuesday." Once again, Father O'Reilly ripped into a straightaway.

"Are you ready to die this very instant? Were you on time for mass this morning? Have you been paying attention every moment to what has been going on up at this altar? Have you been keeping God's laws? Have you been saying your morning and evening prayers? Have you been taking care of your family? Have you been going to Confession every week? Have you have you have you?" Out of the straightaway and climbing again.

"Sometimes you just can't get a man to come to church and when you finally do, it takes six men to get him through the door. We're all going to die, you know. And in a very short time." CLIMB CLIMB CLIMB "We live sixty, seventy, eighty years at the most. It's not a very long time." CLIMB CLIMB CLIMB "Ask someone who's that old. He'll tell you. It just didn't seem to take him that long to get old." CLIMB CLIMB CLIMB "This life is just a testing period. A time for God to see . . ." CLIMB CLIMB CLIMB "if we deserve to spend eternity with Him, to be forever in the presence of His . . ." CLIMB CLIMB CLIMB "beatific vision, to be with Him forever in the happiness of Heaven or . . ." PLUNGE "to be damned for eternity in the everlasting fires of Hell." As we continued to roll on with Father O'Reilly, heads began turning purple from the rapid changes in altitude.

On the way home from mass, Depki stopped in at Marty's Food Shop for his usual entrée of Pepsi and Hostess Twinkies. Lanner, awed by the horrors of the ride his soul had just taken, had stayed for another mass. Even Johnny Hellger, whose mouth normally observed no Sunday blue laws, was unusually quiet. I kept catching my tongue saying silent "Hail Marys." I was going to ask Depki for one of his Twinkies, but I didn't think it would mix too well with the ashes of Hell that were still smoldering in my mouth.

"You know," said Depki as he popped the Pepsi bottle from his mouth, "what if Father O'Reilly's wrong?"

"What do you mean?" I asked.

"What if he's wrong about the whole thing?"

"I don't follow you," I said. Depki shrugged and took another bite of his Twinkie.

"Yeah," said Johnny Hellger, "but what if he's right."

St. Bastion Parish was long overdue for a new church when, at one of his eight o'clock masses, Father O'Reilly announced that the building of a new one was to begin in six weeks. Anyone who was interested in the details was to come to a parish meeting in the school basement the following Tuesday night. Father O'Reilly never discussed money matters from the altar. That's what parish meetings were for.

At the meeting, most of the questions about the new church were asked by the younger couples who had been in St. Bastion Parish for only a few years.

The older couples had learned long ago that Father O'Reilly either did things very right or very wrong and that he was little influenced by what anyone else thought. They were just there to offer their help.

"Where do you plan on putting the new church, Father?" asked a thirty-three-year-old insurance man who felt that being active in one's parish was important to the well-being of one's soul, family, community, and insurance accounts.

"Over on 111th Street," said Father O'Reilly. "It's the only vacant piece of property the church owns. The old church is going to be turned into classrooms, which we badly need."

"Then I presume," said the insurance man, "that you have already started legal proceedings to buy the brown-shingled two-flat on the corner." The insurance man began to sit down.

"You presume wrong," said Father O'Reilly, and the insurance man began to stand up while he was still beginning to sit down.

"You mean," said the insurance man, "she refuses to sell."

"I wouldn't know," said Father O'Reilly. "I haven't asked."

"You mean to tell us, Father, that you plan on building our two-million-dollar church next to that two-flat shanty? Why that place doesn't even have indoor plumbing."

Father Verga, who was standing at a safe distance behind Father O'Reilly, replied, "Our church will have two bathrooms so you don't have to worry about having to run next door."

No one laughed. Father Verga didn't expect anyone to. Father O'Reilly turned around and glared at him. Father Verga's eyes refused to accept the challenge and skipped about the room as if totally unaware of the crime just committed by the mouth below.

Father Verga knew he had sinned grievously. First of all, for attempting to be funny. With Father O'Reilly, God and laughter never mixed. And secondly, for discussing matters of sex, i.e., bathroom, in a mixed group. Father Verga knew he was going to Hell and prayed every night that he'd burn for a better reason than the sins he had committed that day.

Father O'Reilly turned his attention back to the audience.

"That building and its occupant have been there on that corner for a long time. Even before St. Bastion Parish. No one's ever been bothered by it. I doubt if anyone ever will be. Now, as far as I'm concerned, the matter is closed."

"Well, it's not closed as far as we're concerned," said the insurance man. "We're not having our church built next door to Garbage Lady Annie's house." His mouth had said the words "Garbage Lady Annie" before his mind had had time to censor them. Embarrassed at having said a name that only the children of the neighborhood normally vocalized, it was considered beneath the dignity of an adult to say the old lady's name out loud, the insurance man grabbed his wife's hand and bounded out of the basement hall. About twenty other young couples got up and followed him out.

Father O'Reilly watched them leave and then looked at the older couples who had remained. "Now, where were we?" It was the first time that Garbage Lady Annie made the minutes of a St. Bastion Parish meeting.

Garbage Lady Annie was a little dented and demented old lady who dressed in tennis sneakers and old babushkas and dresses that she picked out of people's garbage cans. If it hadn't been for the dresses and babushkas, she could have just as easily been thought of as an old man. Garbage Lady Annie had long ago ceased to appear as, or cared about being, a member of either sex.

Garbage Lady Annie's house resembled a shoebox on its side: long, narrow, porchless, and even with the street level. The building leaned eastward or westward, depending on which way the wind was blowing. Garbage Lady Annie supposedly lived on the first floor because there was a For Rent sign, turned yellow with age, in a window of the second floor. Next to the house was a black dirt yard enclosed by a fence made out of the sides of crates. The yard was loaded with the neighborhood's refuse: piles of newspapers, broken dolls, mismatched boots. Each commodity was neatly stacked in a section of the yard.

No one had ever actually been in Garbage Lady Annie's house. Theories of its contents ranged from more neatly stacked garbage to millions of dollars being stashed in the furniture and linings of the walls. Garbage Lady Annie herself was never actually seen going into or coming out of her house. She did, I'm sure, but no one ever saw her.

Garbage Lady Annie could be seen in only one of two places: in the alleys looking for garbage or in the last pew of St. Bastion Church.

She was strictly a seasonal Catholic. The colder it got, the more of a churchgoer she became. In the worst winter months, Garbage Lady Annie became so religious that she'd often attend all six Sunday masses. You always knew when Garbage Lady Annie was in church because she'd park her red coaster wagon, which she constantly dragged behind her, outside on the church steps.

Many of the women in St. Bastion Parish wished that Garbage Lady Annie had been a little more nonreligious. There was the Sunday morning Garbage

Lady Annie showed up for mass in an old dress that belonged to Depki's mother. Garbage Lady Annie had apparently picked it out of the Depki garbage can. Depki said that for years afterwards, every time his mother wore a new dress, she kept imagining that she was hearing people say, "Yes, yes, that's a very nice dress. I'm sure Garbage Lady Annie will like it."

Most adults thought that Garbage Lady Annie was nuts. I liked her, especially when I was a little kid. Most of the little kids did. She was the only adult we knew who spent most of her time in alleys. As any kid knows, alleys are the best part of a neighborhood.

The dogs of Seven Holy Tombs hated her. Being typical middle-class dogs, they had little to justify their existence. So whenever Garbage Lady Annie started picking in the family garbage can—which was usually located a few feet outside the fence in the alley—the resident dog felt obliged to leap up against the fence and carry on like he'd really bite her if he got the chance. I doubt if there was a dog in the neighborhood who would have risked his health by biting Garbage Lady Annie.

The only dog around who didn't bother Garbage Lady Annie was Blink, a brown lump of matted fur who wandered around the neighborhood. No one knew, or cared, where Blink came from.

Blink could always be found at some neighborhood sporting event: a street-corner softball game, a football game at the park, or a game of marbles being played on a curb. Blink would never bark, run after the ball, or in any other way annoy those around him. He would simply do what he had come to do: watch.

According to Depki, Blink was the great neighborhood protector who regularly ate up other dogs and cats that were mean and kept the neighborhood free of bullies. Depki watched too many Rin Tin Tin movies. I never knew Blink to show any emotion whatsoever. As far as bullies were concerned, the neighborhood was overrun with them. Everyone was bullying somebody.

Although Blink had four legs and a tail and looked exactly like a dog, he wasn't actually considered a dog. You would never walk up to Blink and pat him on the head or say something stupid to him like, "Here Blink, boy." People would have thought you were crazy.

Blink had no yard to "protect," no family to impress. He never bothered Garbage Lady Annie for they were two of a kind.

Garbage Lady Annie was a fixture of the neighborhood just as much as the traffic lights on 111th Street and she warranted about as much attention until the site of the new church was announced.

The insurance man and his followers formed an organization, gave it a sincere title, something like "Concerned Parents for a Better St. Bastion Parish," and set out to denude Garbage Lady Annie of her shanty.

They asked the Chicago Board of Health to force Garbage Lady Annie off her property. The board said there were no legal grounds under which condemnation proceedings could begin. They asked the city Building Commission to condemn the building. The commission told them that Garbage Lady Annie's house had passed a city inspection the previous year. The insurance man and his followers circulated a petition stating that Garbage Lady Annie and her garbage-picking habits were a health hazard to the neighborhood. The petition got "lost" in City Hall. Apparently, the insurance man and his followers had underestimated Garbage Lady Annie's political clout.

They were getting desperate, so desperate they were willing to try anything. They went to talk to Garbage Lady Annie herself.

With his followers standing a safe distance behind him, the insurance man walked up to Garbage Lady Annie's house and gingerly knocked on the front door. It was perhaps the first knock ever laid on Garbage Lady Annie's door. But there was no answer.

They found her picking garbage in the Larding Street alley. There, they asked her if she would like to sell her house. They told her they planned on raising the money for the purchase by holding a cookie drive. Garbage Lady Annie thought they were nuts.

By now the church was finished. A husky red brick bastion with a muscular marble interior. Plain but strong. Though few were overawed by it, everyone seemed to like it. Even the insurance man and his followers agreed that the new church was quite good enough. Garbage Lady Annie was sufficiently impressed. That year, she was seen attending mass as late in the cold season as the last week of March.

Then, there was a fine Catholic tradition, at least on the South Side of Chicago, that after a pastor had completed such a tremendous task as building a new church, he would die shortly thereafter, supposedly because he had worked himself to death completing the job. Father O'Reilly, who was never one to buck tradition, promptly died two months after the new church was completed.

Garbage Lady Annie lived five more years. They found her one Sunday afternoon after the twelve o'clock mass, hunched over in the last pew. The ushers had become suspicious because the day was warming up.

The insurance man and his followers volunteered to examine and dispose of Garbage Lady Annie's house. The insurance man was the first to step inside it. Today, his name is better known in Seven Holy Tombs than is Neil Armstrong's.

On the first and second floors were a few pieces of

old furniture and some piles of junk, neatly arranged, just as there were in the yard. But in the basement, they found a number of large chicken coops filled with chickens. The farmer who came to take the chickens away said that they were Round Neck chickens, a breed of chicken rarely found in this country.

V   Some Great Moments in Sloppy Scouting

Contrary to popular folklore, Cub Scouts do not spend all their time helping old ladies cross the street. In my neighborhood, they couldn't have. There weren't enough old ladies to go around. Larry Gogel, who lived a few doors down from me, owned one. She was his grandmother, I think. All she ever did was sit in the kitchen. She had no desire to cross the living room much less the street.

In the neighborhood of Seven Holy Tombs, Cub Scouting was a lot more than simply collecting bundles of old newspapers on Saturday mornings. It was the training wheels of life and was as much a part of growing up as breaking bones and getting pimples. There was something wrong with a boy's glands if he didn't become a Cub Scout. Boys who didn't join Scouting seemed to grow up strangely. But then, how can you expect a kid to mature properly when he's never dressed like an Indian?

It was Sunday afternoon and my eighth birthday, the age when one normally joins the Cub Scouts. I was due to be initiated into the Scouts the following day. As I walked through the kitchen, my mother told me that my father, who was outside in the backyard painting the fence, wanted to see me.

The first eight years of my life had been somewhat less than impressive. In school, I had started out in the highest reading group, the Robins, but was quickly demoted to the Sparrows. My nun once remarked that she was thinking of creating a new group just for me called the Droppings. My mother made me quit the Pee Wee Baseball League because I kept getting lost on the way home from the park. I even got the feeling that some of my imaginary friends considered me a loser.

When I got to the backyard, my father was squatting next to the fence, painting the pickets.

"You wanted to see me, Dad?" He didn't look up. He just kept painting.

"Yes, son," he said. "Tomorrow is a real big day in your life, as you know. Tomorrow night, you'll wear the blue and gold uniform of a Cub Scout. Your mother and I feel this is a very important step in your life. It's a sign that you're maturing, that you're growing up. You know what I mean, son?"

"Yeah, Dad, I know what you mean." I leaned on the fence.

"I realize that things in the past have not always worked out for you," my father said as he continued to paint the fence, "but I'm sure that as a Cub Scout, you're going to make everyone very proud of you." He looked up from the picket he was painting and saw me leaning on the fence.

"Hey, get your hand off the fence. I just painted there."

I jerked my arm away and looked at my hand. It was loaded with paint. "Sorry, Dad."

He mumbled something about illegitimacy and went back to painting the pickets.

My father was right. I had blown the first eight

years of my life. It was time to grow up. I went next door to find out from Demented David, who had already been a Cub Scout for two years, how one went about making it big in the Scouts.

"Nothin' to it," Demented David told me. "All you have to do to impress your parents is to get Mr. Barnum, the pack leader, to think you're a hotshot. Do a nice job in something, like singing or hiking. If Mr. Barnum notices you, at the next pack meeting he'll lead the whole pack in giving you three cheers." Demented David demonstrated, flinging his fist into the air each time he yelled, "Hip hip hurrah, hip hip hurrah, hip hip hurrah. Most of the parents go to the pack meeting," Demented David continued, "and when they hear their kid getting hip hip hurrahed, they go wild."

"What's a pack?" I asked.

"All the Cub Scouts in each neighborhood make up a 'pack,' which has as its name a four-digit number," Demented David said. "Then each pack is divided into a number of dens made up of nine or ten guys and a den mother."

"And all I have to do to get hip hip hurrahed at a pack meeting is to have Mr. Barnum notice me doing a nice job in something?"

"That's all," said Demented David.

The pack meeting that Monday night was held in the park-house. The meeting began with the Pledge of Allegiance and then Mr. Barnum handed out badges to about twenty different Cub Scouts. After each Cub Scout received his badge, Mr. Barnum would yell, "How about three cheers for . . ." (whoever it was) and while punching our fists into the air, we'd all yell, "Hip hip hurrah, hip hip hurrah, hip hip hurrah." After about forty thousand "hip hip hurrahs," Mr. Barnum welcomed us new Cub Scouts.

"As Cub Scouts, boys," said Mr. Barnum, "you will acquire many new skills that you, as an adult, will need later on in life. You'll be taught to make model airplanes, shoeshine kits, and Mother's Day cards. You will learn how to survive in the wilderness with nothing but two sticks and a Clark Bar."

Mr. Barnum went on to teach us the Cub Scout pledge, sign, handshake, and the secret writing. Mr. Barnum also told us about the three Cub Scout books: the *Wolf Book*, the *Bear Book*, and the *Lion Book*. We would receive badges for completing the exercises and challenges in each book, Mr. Barnum said. Actually, the books sounded like parents between covers.

Mr. Barnum also informed the new members of Pack 3838 that they key word in Cub Scouting was "akela," which was the "secret" word used to refer to a good leader. A good leader included Mr. Barnum, den mothers, parents, and basically anyone taller than a Cub Scout.

"Of course," said Mr. Barnum, "as Cub Scouts you will be trained to be good followers. Good leaders," said Mr. Barnum, "are good followers."

Later in life, I discovered that statement to be untrue. Good leaders are rotten followers because they're always gunning to be leaders.

"Now," said Mr. Barnum, "we're going to do something that all Cub Scouts love to do, sing." He held up his hands as if he were allowing them to drip dry. "And remember, men, use those hands to express the words of the song."

This was what I had been waiting for: an area of skill in which I could immediately establish my supremacy. I limbered up my fingers, ready to perform to perfection the dictations of the song.

Mr. Barnum started us off. "One, two, three . . ."

Do your ears hang low,
Do they wobble to and fro,
Can you tie them in a knot,
Can you tie them in a bow.

Can you throw them over your shoulders
like a Continental soldier, do your ears hang low.

That is not an easy song in which to excel. At first I was panic-stricken. I couldn't do any of the things the song said. My ears didn't hang low, they didn't wobble to and fro. I couldn't tie them in a knot or tie them in a bow. I looked around at the other Cub Scouts. They weren't doing any of those things either. They were just waving their hands around their ears as Mr. Barnum was doing up in front of us.

The next song consumed by our lungs was the national anthem of all Cub Scouts, the "Itsy Bitsy Spider" song.

The itsy bitsy spider ran up the water spout,
Down came the rain and washed the spider out.
Up came the sun and dried up all the rain,
And the itsy bitsy spider crawled up the spout again.

We sang the "Itsy Bitsy Spider" song about fourteen times, each round faster than the previous one. This entire song is accompanied by intricate finger movements, none of them obscene. Such intricate finger movements are not learned in one night of "Itsy Bitsy Spider" singing. Considering I was a novice, I did fairly well except when "the itsy bitsy spider ran up the water spout." I almost broke my thumb. You do not get cheered for that, not even in the Cub Scouts.

I was assigned to Mrs. Dunnewater's den and a week later attended my first den meeting.

Mrs. Dunnewater was perhaps the only woman in the world to ever earn a double-figure income as a crossing guard. She had a habit of throwing herself in front of cars and collecting the insurance money. People became suspicious when she managed to get herself run over on a Saturday afternoon. After suddenly finding herself retired from the crossing-guard force, Mrs. Dunnewater, her fortune made, turned philanthropist and became a den mother for Pack 3838.

Demented David was in my den. He was convinced that the Cub Scouts were destined to become a military power and, marching to the "Itsy Bitsy Spider" song, go off and totally annihilate the Girl Scouts from the face of the earth, among them Demented David's older sister, who, I admit, deserved to be annihilated. Two other members of the den were Bobby Felgen, a massive piece of flesh whose personality was very much like those who leave money under your pillow when you lose a tooth, and Anthony Trielli, who wanted nothing more out of life than to be vice-president of the United States.

At the den meeting, Mrs. Dunnewater announced that Pack 3838's candy drive was beginning. We could pick up our boxes of candy at the next meeting.

This was my chance. I would become a super salesman and lead the pack in selling Cub Scout candy. No doubt I would be rewarded by a standing ovation of three cheers at the next pack meeting. I realized that this would be no minor achievement as Cub Scout candy tasted like chocolate-covered grease. But I knew I could do it. Besides, I had a lot of relatives living in the neighborhood.

On the way home from the meeting, I told Demented David of my plans.

"Forget it," he said, "you'll never beat Alex Schietzer."

"Why? Does he have that many relatives in the neighborhood?"

"No," Demented David said, "he can actually sell the stuff to total strangers. Really, I've seen him. He gets this sappy look on his face and just about cries on the front porch if someone says no to him."

It wasn't even close. Alex beat me by forty-seven boxes and three hip hip hurrahs.

Demented David told me that occasionally Pack 3838 gave three cheers to a kid who behaved particularly well on a field trip. Three weeks later, I had my opportunity when Pack 3838 visited Lincoln Park Zoo.

I had never been to a zoo. The only animals I was familiar with were dogs, cats, and squirrels from a distance. At Lincoln Park Zoo, I discovered just how messy real animals could be about themselves. I spent the entire day holding my nose and/or stomach. Still, I might have had a chance to impress Mr. Barnum with my excellent behavior if I hadn't been given Charley Goodwell as my "buddy."

Any time that Cub Scouts venture out into the world, they are always paired off into groups of twos, or "buddies." Scout leaders will tell you that the idea behind it is for each kid to keep track of his "buddy" and therefore increase the chances of getting everybody home alive. But a Scout leader I knew in my later years told me the true reason. Like all organizations that wear uniforms, the Cub Scouts want to be well organized and keep everything neat and orderly. With the "buddy" system, they figure if one kid gets killed or lost so will his "buddy" so there'll still be even lines on the way home.

Charley Goodwell, being my "buddy," had to sit next to me on the bus as we started home from Lincoln Park Zoo. As will happen on any bus that is loaded with Cub Scouts, some weirdo started singing "100 Bottles of Beer on the Wall" and the rest of us picked it up. As usual, by the time the song got to the low eighties, everyone had quit. Everyone but Charley Goodwell. Charley had only one virtue, persistence. When Charley Goodwell started "100 Bottles of Beer on the Wall," Charley Goodwell finished "100

Bottles of Beer on the Wall." Somewhere around "28 bottles of beer on the wall . . ." I tried to strangle him. At the next pack meeting, I did not receive three cheers for my efforts. Charley Goodwell did for being the most enthusiastic Cub Scout on the field trip. Hip hip hurrah, hip hip hurrah, hip hip hurrah.

Every year, Pack 3838 marched in the Fourth of July parade. Mr. Barnum always gave an award, and three cheers, to the Cub Scout who was the best marcher or, as Mr. Barnum said, "demonstrated the best cadence." That year, I was determined to win it. I needed the three cheers.

For an entire week before the parade, I practiced marching in the backyard. In order to simulate the actual marching conditions of a parade, I got up early one morning before school and marched in the deserted street in front of my house. I was unable, however, to simulate the marching conditions created by walking directly behind an elephant, which was where I marched that Fourth of July. Marching elephants have a way of destroying one's cadence. Fortunately, at the next pack meeting, the elephant did not receive three cheers for his efforts. Unfortunately, neither did I.

In late August, Pack 3838 held its annual Pow Wow Weekend. Pow Wow Weekend was a time when all good Cub Scouts and their parents left the comfort of their homes to dress up like Indians and spend two days in a flat-chested, pock-marked forest preserve. It was forty-eight hours of dodging falling tent poles and two-hundred-pound mosquitoes while consuming metallic well water, warm pop, cold hot dogs, and charcoal-coated hamburgers.

During Pow Wow Weekend, there were two excellent opportunities to earn three cheers. The first was in the softball game against another Cub Scout pack, Pack 3841. The second opportunity came at the very end of the Pow Wow Weekend, when the Indian-dancing contest was held.

There was little chance to grab glory in the softball game. Our pack leader, Mr. Barnum, didn't believe in having anyone ride the bench, so he played everyone in the pack for the entire game. Instead of nine men on the field, we had seventy-five.

In the first inning, thirty others and I were standing in left field. A fly ball was hit right at me. As is customary in the softball world, I yelled, "I've got it," so that no one would run into me. Simultaneously, I heard seventy-four other guys rushing at me yelling, "I've got it." No one got it.

I didn't get to bat. With seventy-five kids in the lineup, the average player got to swing a bat for Pack 3838 once every two years.

We lost, 33 to 12, a relatively tight game by Cub Scout standards. Naturally, we gave the other team three cheers for beating us to death. Hip hip hurrah, hip hip hurrah, hip hip hurrah.

The softball game was played on Friday night. Saturday and Sunday of Pow Wow Weekend progressed smoothly. Only three kids had to be carried off by ambulance. Two of them ran into trees and the third kid managed to swallow the apple during the apple-bobbing contest.

All kinds of things went on during those two days: gunnysack races, pie-baking contests, tugs-of-war. But I was after bigger things. I spent the two days inside my tent practicing my Indian dancing in preparation for the Indian-dancing championship that was to be held Sunday night at the close of the Pow Wow Weekend.

A rigid training schedule was followed. First, I would spend twenty minutes Indian dancing: my body crouched appropriately, the head bobbing, the tails of the Indian headdress weaving behind my back, the mouth producing perfect Indian grunts as my hand rhythmically shuttered over it, and the gym shoes shuffling smoothly under my body. The next twenty minutes would be spent doing push-ups and running around the tent. Conditioning is very important in Indian dancing.

Jerome Bizybinski had won the Indian-dancing championship for the past two years. It wasn't a case of Jerome being so good as it was of Jerome's competition being so bad. Kids who had seen both of us dance said that I definitely had Jerome outclassed. Already I could hear Mr. Barnum announcing me as the new Indian-dancing champion, followed by three lusty cheers from my fellow Cub Scouts. Hip hip hurrah, hip hip hurrah, hip hip hurrah.

I wasted no time during the Pow Wow Weekend going to the outhouse. Unlike the bathroom at home, the outhouse didn't smell of Lysol. Besides the odor, there were hundreds of flies around the outhouse. Most of the guys who used the outhouse held their breaths the whole time they were in there. I couldn't hold my breath that long so I figured I'd just skip the whole process until I got back home.

Demented David warned me that it wasn't a good idea to do that. He had done the same thing the previous year and had gotten a case of constipation that crippled him for two weeks.

The Indian-dancing contest was the climax of the Pow Wow Weekend. After dark, a big bonfire would be built and all the members of the pack would sit in a large circle around it. Each contestant would then stand up and do his stuff. After the winner was announced, the entire pack would Indian-dance around the bonfire. It was a very impressive sight.

The first five contestants were strictly passé. Then Jerome Bizybinski came on. Jerome's dancing was good. Not great, but good. He had a few cute twirls and he kept his head bobbing nicely. But his dance fell far below the routine I was about to unravel around that campfire.

As I was watching Bizybinski dance, I suddenly realized that my legs were turning to concrete. Gastric pains were spreading from the base of my neck to my ankles. My mouth was dehydrating.

Jerome Bizybinski finished dancing and received healthy applause from the circle around the campfire. I tried to stand up but the pain in my stomach forced me into a crouch. Fortunately, a good Indian dancer performs in a crouch so this was no problem. As I shuffled toward the campfire, I noticed the hungry look of anticipation on my fellow Scouts' faces. Word of my skill had spread. They were waiting to witness an upset.

I slowly began dancing. My feet were hardly leaving the ground. I was afraid that if I bobbed my head, it would fall off. There was stunned silence. This was the man who was going to replace Jerome Bizybinski as the Indian-dancing champion of Pack 3838?

Mr. Barnum coughed nervously, stood up, and said mechanically, "Very very good. Now, Scouts, let's sing a few songs around the campfire while the judges decide who is going to be the new Indian-dancing champion of Pack 3838."

A few speckles of applause bid me farewell as I crawled through the circle of singing Cub Scouts and into my tent. I lay coiled on the ground, my Indian headdress hovering over my forehead. Through the blur of agony I could hear them chant.

"The itsy bitsy spider ran up the water spout, down came the rain and washed the spider out, up came the sun and . . . Let's have three cheers for Jerome Bizybinski! Hip hip hurrah, hip hip hurrah, hip hip hurrah."

VI   The Nuns

Many people think of a nun as a shy, petite little thing with a sunshine face pushing out of a habit, playing opposite Bing Crosby in a 1940s movie. In fact, nuns are generally sullen, suspicious cynics with a strong streak of savagery. They aren't at all human. At least not any of the nuns I knew at St. Bastion school.

The St. Bastion nuns couldn't have been human. In my eight years of grammar school, I never saw a nun take a drink of water, go into a washroom except maybe to chase after some kid but never for her own satisfaction, or eat something. As far as I could tell, the nuns were totally devoid of biological functions.

The nuns at St. Bastion school had one goal in life: to get out of it and into Heaven. When they first became nuns, they took three vows that were designed to accomplish this goal: the vows of Poverty, Chastity, and Obedience.

The first vow was easy enough to keep, not only for the nuns but for anyone in St. Bastion Parish. And considering what most of the nuns looked like, Chastity offered no formidable challenge either. The vow of Obedience simply meant that the nuns had to worship the ground the priests walked on, which the nuns did with absolute relish.

By taking these three vows, the nuns at St. Bastion school were among the few souls in the world who knew they were going straight to Heaven. Unfortunately for us kids at St. Bastion's, we weren't a necessary part of their master plan to attain the Eternal Reward. We were simply annoyances strewn along the path to Heaven and were treated as such.

Like most average St. Bastion students, I was absolutely terrified of nuns. Hearing the rattle of the oversized rosary beads hanging from their belts and the stomp of their 1890 black-laced, ankle-high stubby-stacked shoes clapping down the hallway hollowed me with fear. The nuns also had a very strange odor about them, something like kitchen cleanser, that upon entering the nostrils, immediately immobilized one's central nervous system.

You could tell if a nun didn't especially approve of your being alive. She'd address you as "Mr." instead of by your first name. I was always "Mr." Ryan.

A nun didn't like you walking on the stairs at the same time as her. She considered such an act disrespectful and if you forgot and did it, she'd probably knock you around.

The term "kid" was despised by the nuns. I don't know why. Say you found something on the playground, like a glove, and you went into a classroom to try and find the owner. As soon as you held up the glove and asked, "Any kid in here lose this?" the nun would interrupt you. "I'm sorry," she'd say, "but we don't have any 'kids' in here. Just children. Only goats have 'kids.'"

Some of those nuns thought that one-liner was a riot. I guess when you're a nun, it doesn't take too much to amuse you.

The nuns were very smart and very dumb. They were smart in making it a point to know who hung around with whom. At the beginning of a school year, the nuns who were teaching a particular grade would get together and make sure that good friends who were troublemakers would not be in the same classroom.

The nuns were extremely sophisticated when it came to surveillance. If a nun had to leave the class unattended for a few moments, she'd give us some work to do and warn us that while she was gone we had better do the work and not goof around as God, who was everywhere, would be watching. The nun would further inform us that, just in case God missed something, the principal would be listening in on us through the classroom's public-address system.

Maybe God did report back to the nuns. The nuns knew about everything that happened in the neighborhood, which was rather weird since the nuns were never seen anywhere but in the school, the church, or the convent. If you punched a kid in the head on a Saturday afternoon, every nun in the school would know about it by Monday morning.

But in other ways, the nuns were really dumb. Once, when I was in second grade, a nun who was walking by on the playground heard me say "shut up" to some kid. The nun really slapped me around for it, telling me how shocked she was that I'd use such foul language. "Shut up" is just not that big of a deal. Even then, I knew that, and I was only in the second grade.

The nuns also had a dumb habit of presuming that if the first kid in the family who went to school was stupid or smart, then all his brothers and sisters who followed him in school were the same. My older sister had been at St. Bastion Grammar School for two years before I started first grade. She was an excellent student, got good grades, and never misbehaved. She was always helping my mother around the house, wouldn't think of talking back to my parents, was kind to animals, and had won three cooking awards in the Girl Scouts. Naturally, I hated her.

My older sister's reckless behavior had created a family mold that I was constantly failing to fill in the minds of the nuns. They simply refused to admit that glass slippers can't always be passed from one family member to another.

Girls were never bothered by the nuns. I can't recall a girl ever being hit by a nun. The worst that could happen to a girl was to be grabbed by the shoulder and even that was done very gently.

Boys were fair game. Nuns hated boys. Even the couple of nuns who said they liked boys more than girls really didn't. They may have liked boys as much as girls, but not more. The St. Bastion nuns, like most grammar school teachers, were female chauvinist pigs.

In fourth grade, during the first week of school, we had to write essays about what we did during the summer. It was kind of a tough assignment because most of us didn't do anything during the summer. But Mike Depki, who did even less during the summer than most of us, wrote a really good story about what he didn't do during the summer. He told how he hadn't killed anyone or stolen anything, how he didn't get run over by a car, and how he didn't go to Africa. Stuff like that. It was good. I actually enjoyed reading it. It was way long enough, too. Depki's essay covered both sides of a sheet of loose-leaf paper.

I also read Mary Kenny's essay about how she helped her mother during the summer. It was lousy. Mary Kenny got an A, Depki got an F.

First of all, Mary Kenny had a lot of things underlined in red. Nuns love to see things underlined in red. I knew only a couple of guys who underlined things in red and they didn't use a ruler so it looked sloppy anyway.

Mary Kenny also had the initials "J.M.J.," which stood for "Jesus, Mary, and Joseph," on the top of her paper. Nuns expected that. Mike Depki used to put "M.A.D." on the top of his papers until he got knocked around a few times for it. Those were his initials: "Michael Anthony Depki." I have to admit that Mary Kenny's paper wasn't quite as wrinkled as Mike Depki's but his essay sure was a lot better. The truth is that Mary Kenny got an A because she was a girl and Depki got an F because he was a boy.

Although most of us boys got clouted regularly, there were some, usually five or six guys in the classroom, that caught more than their share from the nuns. If, in the first grade, you were identified as "one of those," you were stuck with the label for the duration of your grammar school career. No matter how you tried to change the course of human events, you remained in that category. Mike Depki was in that select slime. So was Johnny Hellger. Lanner and I were borderline cases.

The nuns were always after Johnny Hellger for one reason or another. But having the inside of his desk messy was the thing that most often got him in trouble. All the boys had messy desks. Even some of the girls did. But Johnny Hellger was the only kid who ever got clobbered for it.

We'd be studying for something and the nun, having nothing better to do, would walk over to Johnny Hellger's desk, would lean over, and would look inside to see all the crumpled papers stuck between, on top of, and under the textbooks and workbooks that were piled incoherently in his desk. She'd rip out everything and while Johnny Hellger was trying to pick up all the stuff off the floor, she'd be yelling at him and beating him over the head with one of his own books. Then the nun would warn the rest of the class.

"If anyone else has a sloppy desk, they're going to get the same thing. You've got ten minutes to get those desks cleaned out."

The nun would then send one of her bootlickers up and down the aisles with a wastepaper basket, and as he walked by, everyone would throw in the garbage they had hastily retrieved from their desks.

Those desk-cleaning sessions occurred about once

every six weeks, but they never started without the ritual of roughing up Johnny Hellger first.

Among the faculty at St. Bastion Grammar School was Sister Diane, "Dynamite Diane," so called because of her pestilent impatience. Before coming to St. Bastion's, she had taught at a school for truants in Brooklyn for ten years. Strangely, it wasn't a school for truants when Dynamite Diane began teaching there but quickly became one after she'd been around for only a few months.

Dynamite Diane was six feet three inches tall and had such a small neck that her face seemed to peek like a half-risen sun over the horizon of her massive shoulders. Living proof that even Catholics evolved from apes.

Unlike other nuns who would simply grab a kid by the shoulders and wildly shake him for a few moments, Dynamite Diane would pick up the kid, and the desk if he happened to be in one, and shake until either the victim's head was a virtual satellite orbiting around his neck or he simply fell apart.

Years later, at a cocktail party, I saw two strangers discover that they had both been taught by Dynamite Diane. The two of them slinked off into a corner, survivors of a common campaign, gesturing to one another and chittering in glee at atrocities of Dynamite Diane they thought they had long forgotten.

There were others. Cyril the Savage, who, with either hand, could throw an eraser with speed and accuracy the length of a classroom. She had three basic pitches: a curve, a slider, and a fast eraser, all of them impossible to avoid.

It was a common occurrence for a nun who was teaching us something on the blackboard to suddenly whip around and rifle an eraser at some kid she suspected of not paying attention. It was not a common occurrence for a nun to hit who she was aiming at, the eraser usually pinging an innocent kid. Cyril the Savage, however, was more sportsmanlike than the others, and a better aim. She would always yell a warning at the intended target, knowing full well that the warning would do no good.

Although I never had Cyril the Savage for a regular teacher, she substituted a number of times for my third-grade nun, who was always catching colds in her teeth. When Cyril the Savage was in charge of the room, about every half hour a kid's name would be called out, followed by a quick zip and bonk.

Boom Boom Bernadine liked to grab kids by the ears and bang their heads against the wall whenever they annoyed her. Fortunately for Boom Boom, most of the kids at St. Bastion Grammar School weren't too bright to begin with so if there was any brain damage, it was years before anyone realized it. At the peak of her career, Boom Boom Bernadine got overzealous and ripped an arm muscle while bashing some head against a banister. Never again were her hands to crunch a set of ear lobes. The arm muscle refused to heal. For Boom Boom Bernadine, banging heads against walls was what being a nun was all about. She left the school, never to be seen or heard from again, though there are some graduates of St. Bastion's who still hear her name whenever they brush their hair or otherwise touch their heads.

But all the greats, Dynamite Diane, Cyril the Savage, Boom Boom Bernadine, were strictly minor league when compared to Sister Lee. She had no nickname. None would have done her justice. Sister Lee was ninety years old when I began first grade and she didn't decide to die until I was nearly twenty.

Sister Lee, who taught sixth grade, was smaller than most of her students. She looked about only three feet tall. It was difficult to tell exactly how tall she was because her head was always leaning way over to one side as if her ear was trying to hear what her shoulder had to say.

Lee's body was abnormal not only in its durability and decrepity but also in its appetite for violence, which, even among the nuns, was considered unusually large.

Every summer at the Sunday masses, the priests would ask everyone to pray for Sister Lee because she was dying of a serious disease. It was kind of a stupid thing to say since most people don't die of "nonserious" diseases. Anyway, he'd ask us to pray that Sister Lee had a speedy recovery or a happy death. Each summer, every kid in the parish would pray that she had a happy death and each summer Sister Lee would have a speedy recovery.

In the autumn, Lee would come back to St. Bastion school, her BB eyes zipping back and forth between the corners of the sockets, peering out of that wrinkled face, her tawny lips jibbering to one another with no words coming through the mouth to interrupt them, the fingers of one warped hand rubbing the rosary beads that hung from her belt, and the ear on her bent-over head listening to her shoulder.

The souls of St. Bastion Parish, the nuns, the kids, the parents, the priests, were all bluffers. If you were goofiing around in class or something, the nun might say, "You do that again and I'm going to put your head right through the top of your desk." You knew damn well that if you did it again she wasn't going to put your head right through the top of your desk. The nun might give it a half-hearted try but she wasn't really going to do it. She was bluffing. Or when parents came home from a parent-teacher conference in their usual ranting rage and yelled, "You stupid bum. No more watching television until you're thirty and from now on you can go out to play only twice a year." The clampdown usually lasted for about a week. They were bluffing. Although the kids in the neighborhood fought a lot, punches rarely landed. Each guy would do a lot of jumping around, throw a couple hundred punches, miss with all of them, and end up yelling obscenities at the other guy. They were bluffing.

Everyone sort of became conditioned to this barrage of bluffing that constantly went on. We were all little traffic lights watching the signals of the other fellow. "Green," and everything was okay. "Yellow" meant caution; the bluff was on. "Red," which rarely flashed, meant that someone, somehow, was going to be destroyed. The trouble with Sister Lee was that she had no yellow light. She went straight from green to red, catching her victim totally unprepared. Sister Lee figured that if you killed someone, there was no need to caution him "not to do it again."

Most of us kids would spend the first eleven years of our lives worrying about whether we would get Sister Lee in the sixth grade. St. Bastion's was such a large school that there were four rooms of sixth grade, so the odds were with you. As early as second grade, I remember playing baseball at the park and looking around at my friends, wondering which ones were marked to get Lee. But the summer months immediately preceding sixth grade were the roughest.

I would lie in my room late at night, trying to get to sleep, listening to the summer sounds drifting through my window. I could hear the voices of kids, like Depki and Johnny Hellger, who were allowed to stay out later than me, playing hide-and-seek around the street light. Convertibles with their radios wailing would be riddling down the street while adult conversations floated up from front porches. The day's sun-worn air would linger in my room; the sheets would cling to my skin and I would try to think of a time that I had really ticked off God—an annoyance so immense that it would justify His condemning me to Lee.

But when that September came neither I, nor any of my friends, got Lee. Two weeks after the school year began, though, at Sunday mass, Sister Lee almost got me.

The mass that Sunday morning had started out well enough. I had managed to get a seat at the end of the pew. I love being on the ends of things. In line, I always tried to be either the first or the last kid. And I always hoped I'd get a desk at the end of a row. The big advantage of sitting in the end seat of a pew is that you get a much better view of things, especially if you're sitting on the end near the center aisle.

During a mass, the nuns would walk up and down the aisles, searching for troublemakers or rear-enders, kids who were kneeling but at the same time resting their rear ends on the seat of the pew. When a nun tired of searching, she'd sit down in an end seat of a pew while her eyes would continue to scan the tops of the heads around her.

If a troublemaker or rear-ender was spotted, the nun would leap out of her pew, rush up to the aisle where the offender was harbored, and yell out a threat about how she was going to take care of him the first thing Monday morning when he came back to school. The chances were that she wouldn't since she had yelled threats to at least twenty other kids during the mass and it was impossible for her to remember all of them the next day. But such a threat certainly messed up a guy's Sunday afternoon just worrying about it.

That particular Sunday morning, I was enjoying my terrific view from the end seat of the pew when Sister Lee came up to me and said, "Move it over." I moved it over. She plopped it down.

Masses have always seemed long to me but that was

the first one that lasted over a year. Never before had I been that close to any nun, much less Lee, for that long. I was actually sitting right next to her.

I stared straight ahead at the altar. Like most terrified animals, I was seeking safety by hoping that my body would seep innocuously into my surroundings. I didn't dare look in Lee's direction. That would have really been asking for it.

As the rituals of the mass slowly inched onward, I began wincing every time I heard Lee's rosary beads rattle because I thought she was about to slug me for doing something wrong. I was blinking my eyes too fast. I was positive she was about to punch me for blinking my eyes too fast. I tried not to blink them at all but then my eyes started melting down my cheeks. So I tried squinting them to help clear out the water and then, oh my God, she was going to say something about me squinting.

My hands had become slick with sweat. I looked at them and realized that they were doing nothing but looking back. One must never have hands in church that are doing nothing but looking back. I folded them over one another. I sensed that Lee was about to jab me for the way I had my hands folded. Some nuns are very dogmatic about the way they think your hands should be folded in church. So I folded my hands eight different ways. I knew it. Lee was becoming enraged with me for playing with my hands. At least I thought that she was becoming enraged. Of course I hadn't looked in her direction since she had knelt down. I waited. Nothing happened. Lee hadn't noticed me playing with my hands.

Lee's nunnish odor began scratching through my nostrils. It triggered within me an uncontrollable urge to scratch my nose. I have never been much of a nose scratcher. I have dabbled in it occasionally but it has never become a habit. But at that moment, I had to scratch my nose or go out of my mind. Lee would kill me if I touched my nose. Nuns go crazy when someone starts fooling around with his nose. They get upset if they even see your hand anywhere in the general area of your nose.

I tried scrunching up my face. That only made my nose itch more. There was no sneaky way to do it. If I was three or four kids down the pew from Lee, I might've been able to get away with scratching my nose, but not sitting right next to her.

The itch had tired of waiting for me to relieve it and had begun traveling up through my nostrils, heading straight for my brain. That agitated, unscratched itch was going to kill me right in the middle of mass. There was no choice. I had to scratch fast or that itch was going to blow my brains out.

My left eye rolled to the far corner of its cage, toward where Lee sat next to me. Perhaps I'd get a real break and she'd be looking at someone else for a second before returning to me. My eye strained around my cheek bone. It could see nothing. I angled my head oh so slightly to the left.

Lee was gone. I looked around the church. She wasn't even in sight. I felt the empty seat. Not even warm. My nose didn't itch anymore.

A few minutes later I saw Sister Lee hobbling along, patroling the center aisle. Two kids over from me knelt Paul Logan, a bit of a savage himself. He had a very bad habit of running up behind people he didn't like and hitting them in the head with a house brick. Outside of that, he was a pretty nice guy. He was one of those whose face naturally fell into a smile. He was even smiling when he was hitting someone in the head with a house brick.

During the Offertory of the mass, when we were kneeling, Logan began kicking the underside of the pew with his feet. Every time Lee would sliver by, looking for the origin of the thump thump thump, Logan would quit doing it. So it went.

After mass, we lined up in the center aisle, girls on the left side, boys on the right, and began filing out of the basement church.

The March morning had been damp and cloudy on my way to church. But upon walking out of the basement door, I saw that the day had contracted a premature case of spring fever, the sun having arrived and cured the sky of its blemishes.

Paul Logan was on the second step of the basement staircase when it happened. A black blur suddenly stung him on top of the head. He stopped, momentarily stunned. Logan's right foot hadn't yet gotten word of the attack and was already heading toward the next step. The black blur struck at him again, catching him in the back of the shoulder. Logan staggered forward on the basement stairs, his hands clutching for the top step.

I was two people behind Logan in line. I looked up. Above the stairwell, on street level, stood Lee, her right hand holding her closed black umbrella at the wrong end, putting the walnut hooked handle on the hitting end. Her left hand was fingering the rosary that hung down from her belt.

Paul Logan was on his feet now, having managed to completely navigate the church basement stairs. Lee shuffled over to him and started jabbing the umbrella's walnut hooked handle into every part of his anatomy.

"So you don't like praying to God, do you," Lee said as she jabbed. "Didn't want to tell Him that you were sorry for all the sins you've committed against Him in the past week. No, you wanted to annoy all the people around you while they were trying to pray to God, thanking Him for all He's done for them. But you were too important to pay attention to God. You had better things to do." All the while, Lee kept jabbing jabbing jabbing.

By this time, Logan's face was red from crying. Lee kept telling him how he should ask God's forgiveness for what he had done and how God was all-forgiving and merciful in His love for His children. Sister Lee continued jabbing jabbing jabbing.

Finally, she stopped. Her bent head peeked over her shoulder and the perpetually jibbering lips spat a final sneer at Logan, who had, by now, virtually collapsed to the sidewalk. Lee turned and headed for her Sunday morning breakfast over at the convent.

Walking home with Logan, very slowly as he was still in a daze.

"Why couldn't it have rained?" he said. "Then she would have had to use the umbrella to cover her lousy head. Why couldn't it have rained?" That's all he kept saying to me. Why couldn't it have rained.

And on Sister Lee's breakfast table was Wheaties, the "Breakfast of Champions."

VII   Lent

In Catholicism, the name of the game is pain. The more one suffers, the higher he gets in Heaven. After all, Christ, who began the whole thing, was a great gourmet of pain. He started off by being born Jewish. That, in the eyes of most Catholics, is a fair amount of pain right there.

Christ went through life socially humiliated because no one would believe He was the Son of God and could change water into wine and raise people from the dead. Even in His Crucifixion, His grand finale of frustration, Christ actually lost more followers than

He gained. When He rose from the dead, few of His fellow Jews were really impressed.

Christ led the life of a loser. It was an existence of persistent, pounding, pugnacious, penetrating pain. He was the first Catholic and we all faithfully followed in His footsteps.

St. Bastion parishioners suffered constantly and loved every second of it. Stubbed toes, deaths in the family, cars that wouldn't start, ruptured appendixes, rainy weekends, and scraped knees were all moments of misery that were succulently savored.

According to the rules, the more suffering you did on earth for your sins, the less you would have to do in Purgatory. There were, however, two reserve clauses to this system.

First, the pain experienced must have been beyond one's control. You could not sit around all day banging you heaad against the wall and expect to get to Heaven. Nor could you get credit for the pain experienced by a bad report card since, supposedly, you had control over what went on it.

The second reserve clause stated that the individual must immediately offer up the pain to God. Say you accidentally hit your fingers with a hammer. While the tips of your fingers were still in the process of being pulverized by the head of the hammer, you had to say to yourself, "I offer up this suffering to God." You couldn't swear for two or three minutes and then say, "I offer it up to God." Expediency of intention was of major importance.

Although pain was a year-round pastime in St. Bastion Parish, the apex of agony was those forty days before Easter: the nine hundred and sixty hours of Lent when the pain of simply surviving in St. Bastion's fell far short of the sacrifices necessary for Salvation.

Where the idea of Lent came from, I don't exactly know. It had something to do with Christ having spent forty days in the desert. Fortunately, there were no deserts in Seven Holy Tombs."

Lent was a time of "give ups." At the beginning of the forty days, fathers would give up smoking and swearing, mothers would give up nagging, and children would give up sweets. A few more weeks and we'd all give up.

It was forty days of smiles shrinking into frowns, shortened tempers, and lengthened glares. A time when the tightrope of life became traumatically taut.

About the only people who kind of looked forward to Lent were the fat Catholics. Throughout the Lenten period, everyone between the ages of twenty-one and fifty-nine was allowed to eat meat only once a day. Snacks between meals were also prohibited. In addition, two of the three daily meals could not equal in size the main daily meal. Of course, if you ate like a madman at your main meal, you could still manage, within the rules, to gorge yourself two more times a day and still remain in good standing with the Church.

During Lent, we kids at St. Bastion school had to attend the eight o'clock mass every morning before going to class. On Wednesday and Friday afternoons, we had to go back to church after school and sit through an hour-long Lenten service.

The month of March always managed to fall into Lent. It was a lousy month to exist on the South Side of Chicago anyway, so it was just as well. March was the final fart of winter. It would rain on us one day, freeze us the second day, and on the third day blow us off our feet. By the end of the month, we were globs of wind-wracked ice. In March we would go to school, and the Lenten services that followed, dressed in furlined raincoats, cleated shoes guaranteed not to slide on ice-glazed sidewalks, and bricks in our lunch boxes so we wouldn't blow away.

Latin incantations and burning incense would fill

the air of those Lenten services as we knelt on the unpadded kneelers, our knees dripping blood, our bodies sweltering inside our March suits, and our twenty thousand toes squiggling to get out. We would be kneeling so erect that our spines would be constantly threatening to snap in the middle. But there was no way to take a break. It was impossible to rear-end it through a fur-lined raincoat.

A St. Bastion after-school Lenten service included, among other things, a journey through the "Stations of the Cross." A Stations of the Cross consisted of fourteen illustrations depicting the story of Christ's Crucifixion, from His agony in the garden to the time His body was placed in the tomb.

According to the rules, there had to be a Stations of the Cross in every church. They could be in the form of plaques along the walls of either side of the church, in paintings on the walls, or even depicted in the stained glass windows, but they had to be there.

During the Lenten services, as the priest made the Stations of the Cross, he would stop and stand in front of each station, holding a cross that was mounted on a staff. An altar boy, holding a candle, would stand on either side of him.

The priest's words would meander through our muddled minds as he explained a particular station of the cross, his voice giving emphasis to the pain points. He didn't make any of this stuff up. He read it all out of a little blood-red pamphlet. Each kid in the church also had a little blood-red pamphlet so we could all read and shudder along with him.

I found the story of the Crucifixion an interesting one. Even after hearing it a few thousand times, I still listened to most of it. But after the priest finished telling us what was going on in that particular station, he would then explain why it was going on. That was not so interesting.

"We adore Thee O Christ and we bless Thee," the priest would chant as he quickly genuflected.

"Because by Thy Holy Cross Thou has redeemed the world," we'd all drone in reply as we, too, dropped to one knee.

"The Eleventh Station of the Cross," the priest would cry out as he began reading from the blood-red pamphlet. "Jesus is nailed to the cross. Mary, Holy Mother of Jesus, is pierced anew, as she sees wells of her Son's redeeming blood dug in His hands and feet by the nails of the cross. O Mary, through Jesus' wounds, help me renew my baptismal vows and with those nails bind me to Jesus forever.

"Forgive me O Jesus," the priest would continue to read from the pamphlet, "for I know that it is my sins that have put you on that cross. I realize, Dear Jesus, that each time I disobey my parents, each time I lie, each time I don't listen to the good sisters and priests, I am driving the nails deeper into Your hands and feet."

Besides being held personally responsible for Christ being crucified twice a week, Wednesday and Friday afternoons at three o'clock, each kid at St. Bastion's was expected to "give up" something for Lent: not watching a favorite television show, giving up desserts, or, the perennial favorite, candy.

A day or so before Lent would start, our classroom nun would ask each one of us what we planned on "giving up" for Lent. You'd have to stand up in front of the entire class and tell them what your "give up" was going to be.

In the third grade, the "give ups" were running particularly strong. In the fifth row alone, one kid vowed he would not watch any television during the Lenten period. The kid behind him boldly announced to the class that he was abstaining from desserts at both lunch and supper for the entire duration. It was going to be tough to keep up with "give ups" of that caliber. The dismissal bell rang before the nun got to my row.

"I think," the nun said to us as we began getting ready to go home, "that you should all give up something of real importance for Lent this year to show God how sorry you are for the sins you've committed against Him. Remember, it's your sins that put Christ up on that cross." She looked solemnly up at the crucifix that hung high on the classroom wall and then back to us. "Tomorrow is Ash Wednesday, the beginning of Lent, so tonight is your last chance to tell God what you're going to give up for Him during Lent." The meaning of her words was clear. Don't goof it up.

On the way home from school, I asked myself, Could I give it up for forty days? I looked down at it. My mother had been after me to quit. My father had warned me that if I didn't break the habit I'd be socially retarded, whatever that was. Our family doctor insisted that it was loaded with germs and that I'd ruin my health. My dentist said I'd get buck teeth. But I liked it. It was an inexpensive, convenient, and tasty habit. I thoroughly enjoyed sucking my thumb.

Today, I know my dentist was wrong. My teeth turned out fairly normal. If I hadn't sucked my thumb for all those years, my front teeth would, by now, probably be touching my tonsils.

Most people would say that third graders don't suck their thumbs because they're too old for that kind of stuff and have long ago outgrown such habits. Which is true, for most third graders.

I thought of those Wednesday and Friday afternoon Lenten services, the Stations of the Cross, Christ's Crucifixion, and the blood on my hands. If I gave up sucking my thumb for Lent, I would not only be erasing some of my Purgatory time but I would also be doing my part in getting Christ off the cross, not to mention all the germs I'd be avoiding. The decision was made. The impossible would be attempted. I would "give up" sucking my thumb for Lent.

On the morning of Ash Wednesday, the first day of Lent, the priest placed ashes on my forehead and as he made the sign of the cross with them he said, "Remember man, that you are dust and unto dust you shall return." I presumed that statement included my thumb. It wasn't hard to keep it out of my mouth that day.

Four days into Lent, the imbecilic giddiness characteristic of all new crusaders had been consumed by the panic of withdrawal symptoms. I'd normally spend a few minutes sitting in my little red rocker and sucking my thumb before heading off to school. But without my thumb in my mouth, the little red rocker just didn't seem to rock as smoothly as it had before.

The school day was no problem because, of course, I didn't suck my thumb in public. I wasn't a complete moron. But if it was raining after school and I ended up watching some television, by the third commercial I'd have to sit on my hands to stop my thumb from arching toward my mouth.

After dinner was a tough time, too. There is nothing like following up a good meal with a good thumb-sucking. But the toughest times were at the beginning and end of each day. I always loved to suck my thumb right before I went to sleep and in the first awakening moment of the morning.

I hung on for the first week, though. Not once did I suck my thumb. Those seven days had to have wiped out all of my Purgatory time and then some.

Elation over my total victory of the first week breezed me right through the second week. Then came the third.

I couldn't sleep. My food was tasteless. In school, I had trouble remembering my Catechism questions and

I lost my spelling book. The Wednesday and Friday afternoon Lenten services were beginning to get to me. Big Deal. Being crucified. We all have our crosses to bear. I couldn't suck my thumb, for God's sake.

I tried to think about other things. There wasn't anything else to think about. I tried giving myself pep talks. I had heard somewhere that Notre Dame won a lot of football games because they kept telling their players that any man who played football for Notre Dame had too much pride to allow himself to lose. So I tried that approach. "Come on, kid, you've got what it takes to lay off that thumb until Lent's over. Pride, man, Pride. You've got only three more weeks to go. You can do it, kid. You can do it. Remember Pride, Pride. You said you were going to give up sucking your thumb for Lent and you're too proud to quit. Pride. Pride." Obviously, winning football games was easier than quitting the thumb-sucking habit.

One afternoon after school, I was over at Depki's house while his mother was really giving it to him about never remembering to take out the garbage. She told Depki about how her brother, Depki's uncle, never remembered to take out the garbage when he was young either. It was the only thing her brother had to do when he was a kid, Depki's mother said, but he could never discipline himself to doing it. One thing led to another and now he was living on skid row, drinking out of dirty wine bottles, smoking cigarette butts that he picked off the street, and sleeping in doorways. All because he couldn't discipline himself to taking out the garbage when he was a kid.

It seemed to me that as far as self-discipline was concerned, thumb-sucking and taking out the garbage weren't that different. I convinced myself that if I failed to keep my promise of not sucking my thumb, it would be the first step toward ending up on skid row. It wasn't the idea of skid row that bothered me,

I didn't really know what skid row was. But smoking cigarette butts off the street . . .

I was down to the last week of Lent. The first three days of the week had gone by quickly. For one thing, we had the last two days of the week, Holy Thursday and Good Friday, off from school. Having the last part of the week off always makes the first part of the week go faster.

Holy Thursday was just another free day and, like most, was spent in the pursuit of pleasure: a few hours of street softball in the morning and an afternoon of rolling down dirt hills at a nearby construction site, followed by a leisurely game of marbles. Then came Good Friday.

Good Friday wasn't a good Friday at all. Actually, it was a very lousy one. Since the Chicago public schools were also closed on that day, we Catholic kids couldn't even get the satisfaction of being able to go over and stand outside the public school windows and yell "suckers" to the public school kids inside.

On Good Friday morning, I'd have to go to church and sit with my class for an hour. It was called an "Hour of Devotion." We were supposed to kneel there and think about Christ's suffering and death on the cross.

I'd think about that for the first few minutes but you can't think of that kind of stuff for an entire hour. What I'd actually do is spend a good part of the time staring at the statues with the purple bags over their heads.

At the beginning of Holy Week, the week before Easter Sunday, purple bags would be placed over the heads of all the statues in the church. Why, I don't know. But that really fascinated me. The only time I'd ever look at those statues would be during Holy Week when they had the purple bags over their heads.

Like most Catholic kids at St. Bastion's, I wasn't allowed outside to play on Good Friday between noon and three o'clock, the hours that Christ was being crucified. We were supposed to sit around the house and think about how Christ was suffering and dying for our sins.

My mother had told my sister and me that her grandmother had told her that anyone who said a thousand "Hail Marys" on Good Friday before three o'clock would be granted any three wishes within one year of the said one thousand "Hail Marys." I actually made the thousand "Hail Marys" a few times though on most of the Good Fridays I rarely got past a hundred.

Today, such superstitions don't make any sense. But in those years of blind faith, very little made sense. On the Good Fridays when I said the one thousand "Hail Marys," all my wishes came true.

The only wish I can remember now is when I wished for a new bike. At the time it seemed like a rather outrageous request since my father had already informed me, as only he could, that there was no possible way for me to get a new bike until my sister got one first. Her bike was in much worse shape than mine. Yet, less than three months after the Good Friday on which I had said my thousand "Hail Marys" and wished for a new bike, my father met a friend of his who had a brand-new twenty-four-inch bike that he couldn't use and was willing to sell to my father for half price.

On Holy Thursday, the day before Good Friday, I would make up a list of seven or eight wishes that had been kicking around in my head for the past few months. I would then eliminate all wishes that could wait until the next Good Friday or that I might get even if I didn't pray for them. That would usually get me down to three or four wishes. If one of the remaining wishes was one of mutual interest and benefit, say for the family to take a summer vacation in Indiana, I would ask my sister to wish it for me. She always made her one thousand "Hail Marys." But like most sisters, she was seldom interested in wishes of mutual benefit. So normally I would just forget about two or three of the wishes on my list.

Although I was entitled to three wishes, I really only took two. I figured these one thousand "Hail Marys" were being answered by the Blessed Virgin Mary herself rather than by her son, Jesus Christ. It being Good Friday, Christ must have been reminiscing about His Crucifixion up in Heaven just as we were doing down on earth. He'd hardly be in the mood to listen to some kid's three wishes. Besides, "Hail Marys" were always more or less presumed to go directly to the Blessed Virgin Mary.

So only two of the wishes were legitimate. That is, the primary beneficiary was me. The third was the sugar coating, designed to make the other two more palatable. That one went something like, "Help me be a better person," or "help me get better grades in school." Something far-out like that. Although I realized that once having said my thousand "Hail Marys" before three o'clock on Good Friday, I was entitled to my three wishes, I didn't want to ruin a good thing by getting obnoxious with my requests. I knew that if the Blessed Virgin Mary was anything like my mother, she'd appreciate such a gesture.

In a further attempt to avoid ruining a good thing, I never wished for anything that clearly fell into the category of a miracle. If you think about it, asking for a miracle implies that you're good enough to get a miracle. Christ and the Blessed Virgin Mary might have thought that I was an egomaniac or something if I had made a wish like that and might not have granted me any of my three wishes just to spite me. So although many of my wishes were improbable, none of them was impossible.

I didn't tell any of my friends about the thousand "Hail Marys" and three-wishes routine. I didn't tell Depki because I didn't think he'd believe it. Johnny Hellger might not have believed it either. If he did, he would have taken advantage of it. Johnny Hellger would have done something like using his third wish to wish for three more wishes and just keep it going like that. I might have told Tom Lanner. I don't remember.

One reason I often didn't make my thousand "Hail Marys" on Good Friday was that I would spend a lot of time between noon and three o'clock staring out the living room window at the non-Catholics, watching them playing outside and having a good time. Even some Catholic kids would be out there. Johnny Hellger was. But he was always where he shouldn't have been. Sometimes Depki was, too. But then, it might have been his shift to be on the street so he had no choice.

Beside working on my thousand "Hail Marys," I also used to pray that it would rain between noon and three o'clock so that all those kids would have run and sit inside like me. It happened only once and then it rained only for twenty minutes. It was a spring thunder shower that sneaked up quietly on the neighborhood. As the rain poured down on my street, I patiently waited for the lightning to strike one of the non-Catholics as he streaked for his house. The lightning only struck two trees and they belonged to a Catholic.

According to Catholic tradition, it was supposed to rain on Good Friday while Easter Sunday was always supposed to be sunny and warm. But in Seven Holy Tombs Good Friday was always a beautiful day and it always rained on Easter Sunday. One year the devil outdid himself and we got two feet of snow. It was very strange. Seven Holy Tombs was mostly a Catholic neighborhood, but we always got Protestant weather.

On that Good Friday in third grade, between watching the non-Catholics playing outside and trying to get my thousand "Hail Marys" in, I had no problem avoiding my thumb.

Holy Saturday. The finish line was in sight. In a few hours, it would be Easter Sunday morning and Lent would be over. I was proud of myself and had every right to be. I had met me and I had won. Even then, I realized that victories over such a formidable opponent were going to be rare so I relished it while I had the chance.

I looked down disdainfully at my thumb. Of course, I would continue to suck it after Lent was over, but the forty-day abstinence had proven that I was master. Thumb-sucking would be a pleasure now, not a passion.

Pride. No wonder Notre Dame won so many football games. Pride. I walked around the house with my convex chest and casually mentioned to my mother that she and Dad needn't hide any eggs around the house tonight as I was fully aware that there was, in fact, no Easter Bunny. I had told her the same thing the previous year but she had hidden the eggs anyway and I had searched the house for them anyway. But this year was different. I had now acquired a sense of maturity, a sense of Pride. With such self-dicipline, the world was mine and I knew it. I was tempted to take out my school books and do a little homework. A Saturday first. But, I figured, why overdo it.

After supper, my mother began boiling eggs while my father took out the food colorings and started mixing them in four or five different coffee cups. My sister started spreading newspapers over the kitchen table in preparation for the Easter Saturday night ritual of egg coloring.

I viewed the proceedings with an air of distinguished disinterest and only after my sister had messed up half of the eggs did I relent and, balancing the egg on the wire egg holder, dip it slowly into the coffee cup filled with orange food coloring. I have always had a weakness for orange.

I decided that I would lay awake in bed until midnight when Lent officially ended and suck my thumb for the first time in forty days. Once again I would feel my index finger stroking my nose and my tongue rolling around my thumb. But I fell asleep.

Easter Sunday morning. The purple bags were off. The days of "give ups" were over. For those who had given up on their "give ups" midway through Lent, Easter Sunday morning was a time of endless regret. "Why did I quit?" they'd ask themselves. "Why couldn't I have stuck it out just a little longer? Here it is, Easter Sunday morning already." They would spend the rest of East Sunday deriding themselves, calling themselves lazy slobs, sinners, spineless, all of which were most likely true. But for those who had not given up on their "give ups," Easter Sunday morning was indeed a delicacy.

I woke up and looked out the window. It was raining. Naturally. Then I remembered. I could suck my thumb. With no qualms of conscience whatsoever, I could suck it. Christ had risen from the dead. We were all free.

I jammed it in. Yech! It tasted like a foul-smelling, fat, fleshy fist. I yanked my thumb out and looked at it. There was nothing on it. I stuck it in again and sucked harder. It tasted worse. It didn't even seem to fit right in my mouth. I yanked it out again and stared at it. This couldn't be my hand. This time I tried sticking my thumb in very slowly and then I realized. By winning, I had lost.

Going downstairs and looking through the house for the orange-colored eggs. Wondering why I hadn't heard the Easter Bunny hiding them.

VIII   Bapa and the New York Yankees

I saw it turn into our street. As that black dot in the distance grew into a 1948 black Plymouth coupe, I knew it was him and I knew what he was doing here. Bapa had come to take me to the Promised Land, Comiskey Park, for a Yankee double-header.

It is a fine tradition in this country to name grandparents after idiotic babblings of their grandchildren. I don't know which one of us grandchildren had the distinction of sticking him with the slur, but "Bapa" was the only name I knew the man by.

He was a typical easygoing, cigar-smoking, I'll-give-you-anything-you-want type grandfather. On Saturday afternoons, he'd come over, dragging half of the world behind him. Ice cream, candy, toys, and best of all, piles of unused transfers that he brought from work. Bapa drove a city bus. For the money, not for a living. His living, he said, was done at the ball park and not on the city streets.

You see, my grandfather was a member of a species now almost extinct. He was a baseball fanatic.

Bapa had played some baseball when he was a kid. By his own admission he was not too good and eventually he ran out of teams to get bounced off of. Besides, World War I had come along and tied him up for a couple of years. After he got out, he made the fatal mistake of marrying someone who was not a baseball fanatic. So for the next thirty years or so, Bapa had to be content with simply listening to the ball game on the radio and only very rarely slipping away to Comiskey Park, the cathedral of the White Sox sect, where he was a member.

Although he was upset about Grandma's death, Bapa wasn't so shaken as to miss the afternoon game at Comiskey Park on the day of her funeral. "After all," he commented, "it isn't every day Whitey Ford pitches against the White Sox." My family was pretty concerned about his behavior but I wasn't. Now if it had been the Cleveland Indians playing the White Sox, I could have seen some reason for them getting so worried about him. But the New York Yankees? Who could cast a stone?

No one else in the family particularly liked baseball so as soon as I was old enough to stand and hold a hot dog in one hand without having its weight pull me over, throw out obscenities at the correct time, and learn the proper use of the bathroom, Bapa hauled me off to the ball park.

One Tuesday afternoon, Bapa called me up.

"I've got great news for you, Eddie, can you guess what it is?"

"We're going to a Yankee ball game this weekend."

"Better news than that."

"We're going to a Yankee doubleheader this weekend."

"Even better than that."

"What's better than a Yankee doubleheader?"

"Come on, think."

"I've got it. We're going to a twilight Yankee doubleheader!"

"Right. This Friday night. I'll be by about four-thirty. Make sure you tell your mother you won't be home for supper."

Although Bapa and I had seen a lot of ball games together, we had never managed to catch the almighty New York Yankees in town. Now I was going to see my White Sox go up against them in a nighttime doubleheader. It was too much.

We got to Comiskey Park at about six-thirty, but there was such a large crowd that we didn't get to our seats until after seven o'clock. Batting practice was over and the starting lineups of the two teams were about to be announced over the public-address system. I could see Casey Stengel handing the starting-lineup card to the home plate umpire and then shuffling back to the dugout, his hands in his back pockets.

"And now," boomed the voice of the public-address system, "the starting lineup for the New York Yankees." Such names as Bill "Moose" Skowron, Yogi Berra, Mickey Mantle, Tony Kubek, Hank Bauer, and Clete Boyer echoed and reechoed through every niche in the ball park. The crowd just sat in a dazed silence as those Yankee names badgered their ears and ascended into the night air.

Then the public address announced the White Sox lineup. The only three names I can remember are Sherm Lollar, Nellie Fox, and Minnie Minoso. It was certainly a night of David and Goliath.

The square blobs of lights, stilted high above the ball park, were strewing their brazen yellow offspring over the entire arena, encasing the park in a soft aroma of yellow glow as if the scene were a dream and not real at all.

The White Sox came running out of the dugout to take their positions. Bapa balanced a beer on his knee and while gazing at the field, mumbled through his half-eaten hot dog, "This may be as close to Heaven as I get."

The first Yankee up slammed Bapa and me back to reality as he promptly put the first pitch into the center-field stands. The White Sox were starting some rookie pitcher and it was a pure case of genocide. The Yanks got to the White Sox for three runs in the first inning, one each in the second, third, and fourth innings, three in the seventh, and one in the ninth inning.

The only exciting part of the game was in the fifth inning when, I think, Hank Bauer of the Yankees hit one that was headed straight for the box seats in left field. It was obvious to everyone in the park that it was a home run. Everyone, that is, except Minnie Minoso, the White Sox left fielder, who specialized in crashing into brick walls.

Minnie went racing back toward the left-field wall as if he actually had a chance of catching that ball. He didn't. He barreled into the wall in full stride, making a deadening thud that few actually heard but everyone else imagined. When they carried Minnie off on a stretcher, the crowd gave him a standing ovation.

Ball parks are funny places. You talk to the slob next to you as if he were your lifelong sidekick and you give a standing ovation to some maniac who runs into a wall for no other reason than to get a standing ovation.

As we were standing there applauding Minoso, the guy next to me said, "Jeezzs, that Minoso might not be the greatest ballplayer around but he's sure got a lot of guts."

"Guts maybe," said Bapa as he began sitting down, "but no brains." Bapa was that rare combination of a man: a realistic fanatic.

"Minoso's done that quite a few times this year, hasn't he, Bapa?"

"Five to be exact." Bapa was already concentrating on the next hitter. "Six times actually, but one time

111

Minoso was able to leave the field under his own steam so of course it doesn't count in the official record book. If he can do it twice more, he'll tie Woody 'The Wonder' Wallerson's record of seven unconscious stints set back in 1914. If it hadn't been for extenuating circumstances, Wally could have easily made ten."

"What extenuating circumstances?" I asked.

"After the seventh time, he never regained consciousness. I don't think Wally minded. He set another record doing that."

Bapa, like all baseball fanatics, had a compulsive love of statistics.

By the start of the second game, all the signs of drowsiness were fast encroaching on me. Hot dogs were being consumed in obligatory fashion rather than to quell my appetite. Even sips of beer were being passed up. My eyelids, gaining weight with every moment, fought relentlessly to stay up for it was the second game I really wanted to see. Billy Pierce, my idol supreme, was scheduled to pitch against the devil himself, Whitey Ford. It figured to be a real pitchers' duel and that's exactly what it turned out to be.

For the first seven innings, neither team scored. Then, in the bottom of the eighth inning, the White Sox stole a run.

The first man up, Nellie Fox, fouled off twenty-nine pitches before he finally got a base on balls. The second man up hit the catcher's glove when he swung the bat and got first base on an interference call. Bottleneck Boines, the next man to bat, used the old shirt-sleeve trick.

Bottleneck always wore a uniform eight sizes too large so that if the ball came within three feet of him, it would hit the uniform and he'd get on base as a hit batter. That night, after the ball bumped Bottleneck's sleeve, he put on a stupendous performance of pain, shivering his entire body as if he were about to die of pneumonia.

The White Sox now had the bases loaded with Minnie Minoso due up.

Minnie came out of the dugout looking woozy, obviously still feeling the effects of his last crash against the wall. He played the moment for all its worth, taking his time getting into the batter's box and looking around the park to make sure that there wasn't an inattentive soul in sight. There wasn't. Satisfied that he was the center of all he surveyed, Minnie stepped into the batter's box, dug his back foot in to the dirt, swung at an imaginary pitch, took his stance, and then silently defied Whitey Ford to throw one by him.

Ford reared back and fired one off. Minnie swung so hard he fell down. Strike one! The two of them went through the entire skit again. It was now a no ball, two-strike count on Minnie.

No one in the ball park was worried. Minnie still had one pitch left and that was all he needed to unleash his secret weapon. Whitey Ford wound up and let fly a fast ball. Minnie very calmly stuck his head out across the plate. Whammo! His body spun up like a tenpin, hung for a suspended moment above the plate, and then collapsed to the ground. The half-sheared ball went wobbling down the first-base line. Minnie staggered up, was almost tempted to take a bow, but instead limped down toward first base. That forced in a run and the White Sox were ahead 1 to 0.

The next three White Sox batters struck out and as the game moved into the ninth inning, we led the Yankees by a run. We were three outs away from shutting out the New York Yankees and Whitey Ford. Could this be it? The beginning of the end?

For years I'd heard how the Yankee dynasty couldn't go on forever. But it did. Every spring, sports magazines shouted that this was the year the Yankees would fall. Opposing managers predicted it, newspaper writers hoped for it, and fans begged for it. But the Yanks went right on winning. But maybe losing this game was going to be the first step on a downward journey for the New York Yankees that would carry them from the top of the league standings to a horrendous crush of Yankee pride, ending at the bottom of the American League standings.

No maybe's about it. This was it. And I was there to see it: to witness the first crack in the Yankee fortress.

Ten minutes earlier, I couldn't keep my eyes open. Now I was jumping up and down like crazy. Everyone else was standing up, too. The guy next to me was getting so excited that he was spilling beer all over my feet. I couldn't have cared less. It felt a little sticky between the toes but, through my frequent outings to the ball park, I had become accustomed to Schlitz-scented tennis shoes.

The White Sox came on the field for the ninth inning and bedlam broke loose. The park looked like an open-air insane asylum. As Billy Pierce walked to the pitcher's mound, the fat woman behind me cupped her hands to her mouth and bellowed, "Come on, Billy boy, mow those sonofabitches down."

Bapa was just sitting there, marking something on his scorecard. I leaned down so he could hear me.

"What's the matter, Bapa, too much beer?"

"Nothing's the matter."

"Then why are you just sitting there?"

"How many innings are there in a ball game?" Bapa asked. Already I knew what was coming.

"Nine."

"And how many have they played?"

"Well, eight, but . . ."

"I'll cheer when we win."

At that moment, I realized later, Bapa displayed the

exclusive badge of all professionals: that self-assured serenity that refuses to become unnecessarily excited or to take anything for granted. All professionals have it whether they be baseball fanatics or brain surgeons. Another name for it is cockiness.

The first man Billy Pierce had to face in the top of the ninth inning was Tony Kubek. On the first pitch, Kubek hit a high chopper to the White Sox second baseman, who threw him out by twenty feet. The next Yankee up, Bill Skowron, also swung at the first pitch and lined it right back to Pierce.

The White Sox were now one out away from shutting out the Yankees and Whitey Ford! One out away! One maddening out away! Just one!

Then Mickey Mantle, the cleanup hitter, drilled a single to right field. Two out, a man on first, and we still led the New York Yankees by a run. One more out and it would be all over. Just one more.

Slowly, the Yankee kneeling in the on-deck circle got up and began moving toward the plate, waving four or five bats around his head. His squatty legs had apparently forgotten to keep up with the rest of his body. His beefy shoulders almost hid his neck.

As he stepped into the batter's box, he threw four of the bats behind him and leaned the chosen one on his shoulder. Yogi Berra was ready.

Billy Pierce checked Mantle's lead over at first. Then Pierce pulled both feet together and proceeded to slowly rear back on his left foot, stretching his left arm so far behind him that he appeared as if he were going to knock the center fielder's cap off. At the peak of his windup, Pierce's body became momentarily motionless. An instant later, Pierce started leaning forward, his arm came racing over his head, and his hand released the ball as the windmill lash of his body sped it toward the plate.

The ball was coming in low and outside. Yogi Berra

stood dumb. The ball was almost past him. Suddenly, the springs unleashed in Yogi's wrists, the bat ripped off his shoulder, and the smack of bat on ball migrained through the park.

Minnie Minoso was running back toward the wall in deep left field, looking up with glove outstretched. He had a few fans fooled. They actually thought he had a chance for the ball. But maybe he did. Maybe this time, Minnie Minoso really did have a chance of grabbing it. I looked down at Bapa, still sitting, quite relaxed.

"Upper deck, fifth row," he said.

I looked back toward the field. The ball was just beginning to come down. That familiar thud as Minnie went plowing into the wall and crumbled in a heap at the base of it. The ball landed in the upper deck, fifth row, seventy feet over Minnie Minoso's head. A two-run homer.

As Yogi Berra went into the dugout after rounding the bases, a few of his teammates patted him on the behind as he walked by. None of the Yanks were too terribly excited, though. Pros don't get excited.

Already the crowd was moving for the exits even though the game had a half an inning to go. Bapa wanted to wait.

"Minoso's still down there," Bapa said. "Let's see what happens. Here come the boys with the stretcher. Now we can go."

We started walking down the ramp. By the time we reached ground level, the final score was being announced: New York Yankees 2, and the White Sox 1. I felt as if I was a part of the world's largest funeral. Almost no one was talking.

"Well," said Bapa, "one more time and Minoso will tie Wallerson's record."

"Think he'll make it, Bapa?"

"Oh, I think so. Minoso's got the head for it."

IX *Dirty Shirt Andy*

Dirty Shirt Andy owned what passed for a grocery store on the corner of 103rd and Allen Street. He went under a number of aliases such as "The Slob," "Fat Man Andy," and simply "The Pig." But Dirty Shirt Andy was his real name. No one could wear a shirt as dirty as Dirty Shirt Andy.

A kid never went to Dirty Shirt's unless it was to look for something that was "out." Dirty Shirt Andy always had the stuff that was "out" simply because no one went to him to buy it when it was "in."

Kites in August, marbles in October, and hockey sticks in April. That was Dirty Shirt. His store was about four months behind all the other grocery stores in the neighborhood. In toy turnover, that is.

In food turnover, he had to be at least five years behind. All the food in Dirty Shirt Andy's looked the same. There'd be a little yellow shriveled-up label on one of the shelves that would read "bread." All there would be above it would be large greenish brown lumps. Then on the next shelf there'd be a label that would read "cookies" and above that would be a lot of little greenish brown humps.

The canned food looked the same, too. Silver. None of it had any labels. The only edible stuff in Dirty Shirt Andy's store was his potatoes. They were growing out of everything.

Dirty Shirt's storefront boasted the only ghetto-gray window panes in the neighborhood. Behind one of the panes was a group of ten-year-old comic books, stripped of their covers and thrown around a pile of canned Henrietta's Beets, unlabeled of course. Two of the cans were half opened and Louie Vega, the foremost beet authority in the neighborhood, said they were definitely "Henrietta's." It wasn't a matter of faith and morals, but Louis's opinion carried a lot of weight when it came to beets.

Now everyone knows there's only one source of evil in the world. It's just that no one seems to be able to agree on what that particular source is. Christians claim it's Adam and Eve while non-Christians claim it's Christians. Other speculations have included certain animals, witches, the devil, and politicians.

But in our neighborhood, there was no doubt whatsoever what that one source of evil was. It was Dirty Shirt Andy, though most adults simply referred to him as "that moron on 103rd and Allen Street."

Anything that went wrong in my neighborhood could be traced back directly to Dirty Shirt Andy. If church attendance was down, it was because people were too busy reading the dirty books they had bought at Dirty Shirt's. If a kid was late for school, he had probably stopped at Dirty Shirt's to buy some cigarettes. If a black family was seen driving around the neighborhood, it was because they were looking to buy some old food from Dirty Shirt Andy.

It was so accepted that Dirty Shirt was the one source of evil in the world that if you happened to ask someone in my neighborhood, "What is THE source of evil in the world?" they would look at you as if you had asked, "Is the sun hot?" That's just the way they would look at you.

It was the adults of the neighborhood who held that view, though, and not us kids. Most of us liked Dirty Shirt Andy because he didn't treat us like kids. Adults would like you because you were a kid or would dislike you because you were a kid. Not Dirty Shirt. He hated us because we were people. Child or adult, it made no difference to Dirty Shirt. If you showed the signs of a human being, then he hated your guts. He detested every and all, his hatred refusing to discriminate on the basis of age. Dirty Shirt Andy was truly a democratic hater.

There were a few kids who agreed with the adults that Dirty Shirt was the one source of evil but they were the same ones who took the adult line on all major issues. In short, they were the Royal Pain kids.

I, like most of my peers, was convinced that adults, not Dirty Shirt Andy, were the one source of evil. Until that moment in my seventh year of youth when I became a believer.

On that particular day, my older sister and I were going around turning in empty pop bottles that we had collected from our basement, the space underneath the kitchen sink, and neighborhood prairies. We had got rid of the Pepsis at Ed's Store, the Cokes at Ginny's Food Mart, and had even managed to unload the Nehies at the Midwest. Now we were stuck with some unmentionables such as "Loring Cherry Soda, THE PRIDE OF EAST LANSING." Where else? We headed for Dirty Shirt's.

We walked in and headed down the long aisle toward the back of the store, each of us carrying two cartons of empty pop bottles.

We had to step around Dirty Shirt's dog, a wrinkling, ratty fur slab of a nauseating hue that nobody had thought up a name for yet. Although the dog matched Andy's lust for filth, it definitely had a more pleasing personality. It slept most of the time.

We got to the end of the aisle. There, amid the growing potatoes, greenish brown humps, and old hockey sticks sat Dirty Shirt Andy with his bald head sliced by dirt-crusted wrinkles, the U-shaped frown dangling over the unshaven jaw, followed by a three-inch strip of neck. Then the grand finale. That crud-coated T-shirt vainly trying to shelter Dirty Shirt Andy's preposterous pot.

He was sitting, as usual, behind the counter with the Butternut Bread advertisement stretched across the front of it. "Tut tut nothing but . . ." The "Butternut Bread" was scratched out and an obscenity had been scribbled in.

We walked up and put the cartons on the counter. I was biting my tongue. I was, after all, standing before Dirty Shirt Andy, alias "The Slob," "Fat Man Andy," and "The Pig." But normal human beings don't go around calling people names like that. Especially when that normal human being is three feet tall and the object of his derision is one Butternut Bread counter away and would just as soon kill him as look at him.

But I could feel those words racing up my throat, slithering past my tongue, and bellowing by my teeth. Hey, Dirty Shirt, give us some money for these empty pop bottles, huh?

I didn't have to worry about saying anything wrong. My sister was already starting to speak. She was biting her tongue too, I could tell. And she was mentally checking every word before letting it out, lest she make a fatal slip.

"Hello, Andy. We were wondering if you could give us the deposit money on these empty pop bottles."

Andy began in his Mississippi, South Side of Chicago accent.

"What ya got dere?"

"Oh, we've got all kinds here, Andy."

"I know dat. I can see, ya know. How many? How many?"

"Four cartons, Andy. Twenty-four bottles."

"Forty-eight cents' worth, huh. Tell ya what, I'll make ya a deal."

"What . . . what kind of a deal?"

Dirty Shirt Andy reached down behind the counter and brought up a puppy. A black and white one. "I tell ya what, throw in fifty cents and the pop bottles and he's yours."

"All we've got are the pop bottles, Andy."

"Well . . . okay. It's against my better judgment, but I'll make ya an even trade. The dog for the bottles."

I looked down at the mongrel on the floor and then up at the puppy.

"Ya don't have to worry about that. They ain't related." Dirty Shirt tried to put on a smile but he couldn't seem to remember what one looked like.

My sister and I looked at each other. We knew a good deal when we saw one. That wasn't the problem. It was the hierarchy at home. For years we had been trying to get a dog into the house but every attempt had been smacked down by a logical no. But now we realized that life had pitched one right across the plate. Our eyes silently conferred. It was unanimous. Swing!

"Okay, Andy, it's a deal."

"Put da bottles at the end of da counter and here's your dog."

We scampered the four blocks home. The dog piddled on my sister twice and me once. I stood outside with the puppy next to the side door while my sister went in to deliver the news. Through the screen, I could hear her talking to my mother.

"I see you're home, dear. Get rid of all your bottles?"

"Yes we did, Mother."

"That's nice. How much money did you and your brother make?"

"Ninety-six cents and . . . one dog."

"Oh, that's nice. What are you going to do with . . . What dog?"

"We got a dog for some of the pop bottles."

"From who?"

"Dirty Shirt."

"Where's it at?"

"At the side door."

I heard her coming. Mom flung open the side door and looked at the puppy, which was sitting on my shoes. She stared disbelievingly, as if it were missing two of its heads or something. She knew Dirty Shirt Andy, too.

"It is kind of cute."

"Can we keep it, huh, Ma, huh, can we, huh, can we?"

"We'll see what your father says." We were in. We knew it. She knew it.

My father got home late that night.

"Hi, hon. What's for dinner?"

"Stew, dear."

"Anything new?"

"Why yes. The children got a puppy today."

"Got a what?"

"A puppy. You know, a little dog."

"I know what it is. That's just what we need around here. Four more legs. Where is it?"

"Downstairs in a corner of the basement in a little cardboard box. I gave him our alarm clock."

"Why? Does the damn thing have to get up for work? I do, you know."

"Keep your voice down. The children are listening. Why don't you go downstairs and take a look at the little thing before you get yourself so excited over it."

He walked through the kitchen, past my sister and I, mumbling about how he should have reenlisted, and headed down the stairs to the basement, closing the door behind him. The three of us listened as his feet

122

chewed up each descending step. BAM BAM BAM BAM. My mother's brain had a built-in radar system for my father's temper. It worked on the principle of bams. Loud and slow bams were a bad sign and that was exactly the sound charging up from those stairs.

A few seconds of silence as he walked across the basement. Then, clumping, scratchy, blurry noises as if someone was madly trying to get up the stairs. We opened the door and, sure enough, that's what my father was doing: madly trying to get up the stairs. Finally he made it, slammed the door behind him, and locked it.

All we could hear now was my father's heavy breathing and the tinkling of puppy's paws as they moved up the basement stairs. Slowly, my father began to wheeze out words.

"That . . . dog is . . . foaming . . . at . . . the . . . mouth."

I looked through the keyhole. He was right.

"It's . . . got . . . rabies. . . . Where . . . did . . . you get . . . that . . . dog?"

Where else?

I looked at my sister but she didn't look back. We'd been conned. In my mind, I could see Dirty Shirt Andy leaning over his Butternut Bread counter, bits of dirt crumbling off his T-shirt as it brushed against the edge, summing up the entire situation in the same word that Bugs Bunny puts it to Elmer Fudd. Sucker.

For the rest of my youth, I was a disciple of the good. And like any disciple of the good, I spent all my time telling everyone where the bad came from.

"You wanna know why our school didn't get the day off like the rest of the schools? Because Dirty Shirt Andy talked to our principal, that's why." "You know who told your mother you broke that window? Dirty Shirt Andy, that's who." "Don't you know why it's raining on Saturday? Because Dirty Shirt Andy bumped his head on the end of the bed and couldn't get up in the morning. Don't believe me, huh? Well, have you seen Dirty Shirt this morning? I didn't think so."

Within a few months, every kid in Seven Holy Tombs was converted. It seems that Dirty Shirt Andy had sold more than one foaming dog. Like typical converts, most of the kids simply took their old belief and wound it in with their new one. Adults were still, in general, believed to be the source of all evil. But THE adult source of all evil was Dirty Shirt Andy.

A few years ago, I ran into Louie Vega in downtown Chicago. He's a steelworker now. We both had a little time so we stopped in at a bar and shot the bull about the old neighborhood. Lou still lives there.

"Say, Lou, does Dirty Shirt Andy still have that store on 103rd and Allen Street?"

"No, he moved out about five years ago. The city condemned him. Not the building, just him. Someone's told me he's died since then," said Lou.

"Do you believe it?" I asked.

Lou leaned over the table and in a very hushed tone said, "There's a lot of talk about God being dead, isn't there?"

"Yes, Lou, there is."

"Now take a look around you at this world full of crime, Communists, race riots, beatnik college kids, and all the other kinds of shit that we live in."

I did, but all I saw was the inside of a cocktail lounge. Lou sat up, very satisfied with himself.

"After taking a look at this world, it's not hard to believe that God is dead, is it?"

"No, Lou, not hard at all."

"Now you and I know THE source of all this evil, don't we?"

"Yes, Lou, I guess we do."

"Now take a look at that very same world and tell me that Dirty Shirt Andy is dead."

I didn't have to. Lou was right.

"Never," I replied, "never."

X *Felix the Filth Fiend Lindor*

Like any average human being, I received my sex education in alleys, under stairwells, on street corners, and in vacant lots. I did, however, have the privilege of studying under one of the most fabulously filthy minds of the modern era—Felix the Filth Fiend Lindor.

Felix Lindor had enough dirt in his mind to apply for statehood. He had to have gone through puberty during his preschool years because he was already a dirty old man by the time he got to the first grade. He constantly made snide remarks about "Dick and Jane," and once when we were talking about "Superman," Felix told me what *he'd* do if he had X-ray vision.

Felix the Filth Fiend knew almost everything there was to know about sex and what he didn't know, I later discovered, he made up.

No matter who in the neighborhood told you a dirty joke, you knew it originated in the muddy mouth of Felix Lindor. Felix himself told such dirty jokes that sometimes he didn't even get them. Of course, Felix never did understand jokes with double meanings. He could never find the clean one.

Although Felix was undoubtedly born with more than his share of the sex syndrome that we're all blessed with, he developed his talents with diligence and self-discipline until he drove himself to the absolute depths of depravity. For Felix the Filth Fiend

Lindor, a dirty mind was a twenty-four-hour-a-day job. He could look up at any cloud and see a dirty picture.

I didn't get to know Felix Lindor really well until I was in the fifth grade. Felix lived on the other side of the neighborhood, so I never went to his house or anything like that.

There were a couple of large dirt hills, surrounded by weeds, in a prairie on Roland Avenue. In one of the hills, some kids had dug a small cave. The cave had an extremely small entrance so you really had to squeeze to get through it. The cave was pretty small inside, too. Everyone had to sit with his knees up against his chest.

It was there in that cave that Johnny Hellger, Tom Lanner, and I, and sometimes Depki, would meet Felix after school, two or three afternoons a week.

Johnny Hellger would bring cigarettes—he claimed he was already a pack-a-day man—and would give one to each of us along with a mint Life Saver to kill the tobacco smell on our breaths before we went home for supper. Johnny Hellger was intensely proud of his index and middle fingers, which had turned yellow from holding cigarettes. He often bragged about having the yellowest fingers of any fifth grader at St. Bastion's.

Johnny Hellger could also inhale the smoke, talk a few seconds, and then blow the smoke out through his nose. He could entertain you for hours with a pack of cigarettes.

Hellger never believed that stuff about smoking stunting your growth. Years later, when Johnny was full-grown, he stood just slightly taller than a king-size cigarette.

In my neighborhood you had to be careful what you said to a guy about sex. If you said something that betrayed your ignorance, you'd get pie-in-the-face laughs and be reminded of your stupidity for weeks afterward even though the guys doing the laughing may have gotten the correct information only a few hours before you talked to them. But there is little joy in knowing something unless you can laugh at someone who doesn't.

Therein lay Felix's greatness. He loved ignorance. You could ask Felix any question about sex with no danger of derision. The cruder the question, the better. This mentor of the mundane would lean back, jet-stream the cigarette smoke from his mouth, pick the pieces of tobacco from his tongue, and in his whorish voice proceed to explain, in detail, things we'd never even heard about, diagraming difficult concepts in the dirt with his finger. Felix was a multimedia man when it came to teaching.

Felix Lindor believed in using concise terminology. His definitions never contained words of more than five letters. When the lecture began to lag, Felix would throw in a dirty anecdote, using names of kids we knew. Besides teaching theory, Felix also gave us lessons in social protocol.

"When you take a piss in a girl's house," said Felix, "always bank it off the side of the toilet. Otherwise, it sounds like hell and everyone in the house can hear you taking a piss. It's also a good idea to pull the chain just as you're starting. That way, nobody can hear nothing."

Then there was the day Felix introduced us to the art of buying a dirty book, a feat that was more easily performed then than now.

Today, there aren't many good dirty books around. Obscene ones? yes. But dirty ones? no. Great dirty books, like great lovers, always maintain a certain level of tension in the suitor that keeps him coming back. Only at closing sales should you let it all hang out.

A girl looks more enticing in a tight skirt than she does naked. The same principle holds true in books. The sex act is a rather simple biological function. Stated in clinical terms, it would make boring reading. Therefore, the secret of succulent success for a dirty book is to treat sex as if it were dirty. Lots of description and very little narration of actual sexual acts.

A good dirty book has only about three actual sex acts, each preceded by fifty pages of sensuous description, which, if the proper lines are reread twenty or thirty times, gives the reader a feeling of active participation. Once you have savored a truly dirty book, an obscene book will usually strike you as . . . well . . . obscene.

Obscene books simply, and very briefly, describe one ultimate sex act after the other, leaving nothing to the imagination. Instead of discussing sex as the dirty, disgusting, degrading debauchery that we all know and love, an obscene book talks about sex as if it were perfectly legitimate and clean. Disgusting.

A good dirty book starts off with an innocent kiss on page 3, a not so innocent touch on page 20. By page 135, the heavy action is well under way and by page 150, the details of the score are being narrated. A few pages at the end to state the "moral" of the book so it can be classified as "art" rather than pornography and that's it. The cover of a dirty book is usually simple, with perhaps just the title.

Obscene books, however, have very obscene covers. Within the first two pages, they've done it all. Like throwing an ocean at a thirsty man. Drowning him is not the same as satisfying his thirst.

In fifth grade, when I was listening to Felix the Filth Fiend Lindor in the dirt-hill cave, there was no worry about confusing dirty books with obscene ones. Obscene books hadn't been invented yet and, thanks to Father O'Reilly, even dirty books were hard to come by in Seven Holy Tombs. But for Felix, the Marco of Porno, such logistics problems were easily solved.

After a particularly intriguing lecture in the dirt-hill cave one afternoon, Felix said to us, "If you guys wanna read some good stuff"—we certainly knew what Felix meant by "good stuff"—"you oughta buy some paperbacks at Cormie's Drugstore."

"Cromie's Drugstore? I've never heard of it, Felix," Johnny Hellger said between the circles of cigarette smoke he was haloing from his mouth.

"It's in the Seventy-ninth Street neighborhood, over by the Hollywood Theater," said Felix. "The only stores around here that have dirty books are Dirty Shirt Andy's and Devlin's Drugstore. But if you go to either of those places, you take the chance of someone you know seeing you buying dirty books. But there ain't anybody in that Seventy-ninth Street neighborhood who knows any of us."

"I've never seen Cormie's Drugstore," said Lanner, "and I was at the Hollywood Theater just last weekend." Lanner could hardly talk, his eyes were watering so badly from the smoke of the cigarette he was holding. "Hey, I think I hear something outside." Lanner crawled to the mouth of the cave and cautiously poked his head out.

Both Lanner and I worried that the cave was going to be raided some day, by whom we didn't know. I guess we worried because we knew the cave deserved to be raided.

"Lanner," yelled Felix, who was obviously annoyed by the interruption, "will you quit your fucking around and get back in here."

Lanner resettled himself against the wall of the cave, his eyes still listening for any foreign sound in the prairie that surrounded the dirt-hill cave. "It must have been the weeds blowing around out there," said Lanner apprehensively.

"Yeah, yeah," said Felix the Filth Fiend Lindor. "Anyways, Cormie's Drugstore isn't on the same block as the Hollywood Theater. It's about a block down on Seventy-ninth Street. Say, when are you going to the show next, Lanner?"

"We're both going this Saturday afternoon, Felix," I said. "Hey, Hellger, you wanna come along, too?"

"Naw, I can't. I gotta go see my grandfather. He's dying again."

Felix leaned forward toward Lanner and me, as if the dirt walls were trying to listen. "Look you guys, I'm gonna tell you how to buy some really great dirty books. You wanna know how to buy dirty books, don't you?"

Did we want to know how to buy dirty books? Why else were we huddled in a dirt-hill cave, our eyes smarting from the cigarette smoke, the flesh on our arms being ravaged by invisible bugs, our nostrils wilting from the onslaught of Johnny Hellger's bad breath. Lanner and I certainly weren't there trying to work off Purgatory time.

"Here's what you do," said Felix. "First of all, when you get in Cromie's Durgstore, make sure there's no one in the place that knows you. That neighborhood's pretty far from here, but you never know. So check that first.

"As soon as you get in there, buy some candy bars and then go over to the magazine and book racks. Don't eat the candy bars while you're in the drugstore 'cause that gives 'em the idea that you bought the candy bars just so you could eat 'em while you're looking for dirty books.

"Now, if you walk right over to the magazine and book racks as soon as you get in the store, without first buying some candy bars, the guy behind the counter is gonna figure you don't plan on spending any money so he might ask you to leave right away. But if you show him right off that you're a paying customer, he'll be less liable to throw you out. I know that sounds crazy to you two, but that's the way those guys think.

"When you get over to the racks, remember that you can't spend a lot of time there because if you do you're gonna get bounced.

"Forget about the magazines. No matter how dirty the covers look, they're not worth it. I spent fifty cents on one of those movie magazines once that said something on the cover about Liz and her seven lovers that she went to bed with every night. Exclusive photos, the whole bit. Her seven lovers turned out to be cats. That was fifty cents shot to hell. So remember, forget about the magazines, they're a waste of time.

"Don't bother with any of the detective paperbacks. You're lucky if you can find three dirty paragraphs in one of those books.

"If you look through a book and it seems like the writer's really trying to tell a good story, don't bother with it. If the guy's out to write a good book, he's not gonna have a lot of room for dirty stuff. And also skip over the ones that have the writer's picture on the cover. Writers don't put their pictures on the covers of dirty books.

"What I do is I usually check a few pages at the beginning, in the middle, and at the end of a book. Out of those, if I can't find at least two dirty pages, I figure the books's not worth my time.

"Another thing you can try is letting the book kinda fall open naturally in your hand. A lot of other people have looked through those books too, and maybe they've found the dirty pages already. If that's the case, the book will sometimes fall open to the dirty pages. This trick doesn't always work, but sometimes it does."

"Man, you sure know what you're doing, Felix," Lanner said. Felix threw Lanner a sneer from the side of his mouth, not recognizing Lanner's awe with even a comment.

"Oh yeah," Felix continued, "have even change for whatever books you're buying. The longer you have to stand in front of the counter with those books, the more likely the guy behind the counter will give you a hard time, like asking you how old you are and shit like that. And after you've paid, wait long enough for him to give you a bag to carry the books in. You wouldn't want to be seen on the bus carrying them. You guys got all that?"

"What's in it for you, Felix?" I asked. I wasn't quite as naïve as Tom Lanner. For one thing, I hung around with Johnny Hellger a lot more than Lanner did.

"All I ask," said Felix, "is that I get to read the books after you're through with them."

"Me too," said Johnny Hellger.

"Oh no you don't, Hellger," I said. "If you can't come along with Lanner and me to help buy them, you can't help us read them either."

"For Christ's sake, that's not fair. I told you I gotta go visit my grandfather this weekend. He's dying, for Christ's sake."

"He's been dying for the last three years. How long does he plan on taking?"

"You knocking my grandfather, Ryan?" Johnny Hellger started getting up but when his head hit the dirt ceiling, he remembered that he was in the cave. "I dare you to say that again, Ryan. I double dare you to say that again."

"Double darers go first," I began to reply, but Felix cut short my legal retort.

"All right, all right you guys, let's cut out all this

arguing crap. Now, I think you guys agree that it's fair I not pay anything. I've done my share by telling you guys all this stuff. Agreed? Okay, Lanner and Ryan, you guys should buy one book each. They usually cost about thirty-five cents apiece. Since we're all in this together, I think Hellger should be allowed to read the books after you guys get done with them if he pays a third of the cost." Felix looked over at me. "Fair enough, Ryan?"

"Fair enough."

"That okay with you?" Felix nodded toward Lanner.

"Yeah, okay."

"We'll meet back here Monday after school," Felix said. "You two make sure you have the books with you. Now let's get the hell out of here. I'm getting bitten all over the goddamn place."

About an hour later, Tom Lanner and I were parking our bikes in front of "Mary's" Delicatessen.

"You know, Eddie," said Lanner as we entered the store, "I don't like the idea of going to Cormie's Drugstore tomorrow. That's a rough neighborhood. Usually when we go to the Hollywood Theater, we get off at the bus stop in front of the place and walk right into the show. But Felix said Cromie's is at least a block away. I'm not looking forward to walking around there."

"I don't like the idea either, Tom. But I don't see any way out of it."

"There's a good show at the Hollywood Theater tomorrow, too," Lanner lamented, "*Savage Sundown*. And we won't be able to see it because we'll be spending all our time getting those books."

I was now standing over "Mary's" Delicatessen's freezer chest, searching under the frozen packages for a couple of ice cream cones.

"You wanna go tell Felix that we're gonna back out of it?" I asked.

"Not me, man. How about you, Eddie?"

"Chocolate or vanilla, Lanner?"

"Chocolate."

In big black letters, the marquee of the Hollywood Theater announced *Savage Sundown*, starring some people whose names I don't remember. I could see the same actor three weeks in a row and still not be aware of his real name. Sometimes I couldn't even tell whether the guy on the screen was the same guy I'd seen in a different movie the previous week. I'm still that way.

As Lanner and I got off the bus, Lanner looked up at the marquee and said, "Why don't we tell Felix we lost the money?"

"He'd never believe us, Lanner. Come on, let's get it over with."

I was beginning to feel lousy about the whole situation. For one thing, I really enjoyed going to the movies with Lanner. He saw more than most people did. Six months later, he could recall almost every scene in a movie. I couldn't do that the next day. In horror pictures, though, Lanner hardly saw anything at all.

Whenever a scary part came on, Lanner would simply get up and walk out into the lobby, coming back to his seat only when he was sure the scary scene was over. He was the only kid I knew who had enough guts to do that.

Johnny Hellger would run out into the lobby, too. But he was always making up excuses, like he had to go to the washroom or get some candy. A lot of kids pulled that "excuses" stuff. Not Lanner. If he was scared, he'd tell you so.

I myself was never much impressed by horror pictures. Everything else in life terrified me, but not horror pictures.

As soon as Lanner and I turned the corner, I spotted a Prescription Drugs sign hanging over the sidewalk at the far end of the street.

"That Prescription Drugs sign must be Cromie's, huh, Tom?"

"Yeah, I guess so."

The Seventy-ninth Street neighborhood, occupied mostly by feeble red stone apartment buildings, was a much older neighborhood than Seven Holy Tombs. Seventy-ninth and Kenian, the street that the Hollywood Theater was on, was a nice-looking street. But the same could not be said for the street on which Lanner and I were looking for Cromie's Drugstore.

Little shops with slimy windows seemed to shove at you as you walked by them. The curbs were crummy with garbage while used chewing gum soured the sidewalks and obscenities sprawled across boarded store windows. The people walking by didn't look so hot either.

"I sure wish Cromie's wasn't way the heck on the other end of the street," said Lanner.

"So do I, Tom, so do I."

We walked hurriedly toward the Prescription Drugs sign, our feet automatically weaving through the used gum on the sidewalk. Some old guy carrying a bottle of booze teetered up to us and mumbled something to Lanner. We couldn't understand what he said, but we sure started walking a lot faster.

As we opened the door to Cromie's, a tiny bell clanged overhead. The moment it clanged, Lanner shoved into me from behind. I yelled at him over my shoulder.

"Will you watch where you're going, Lanner. Relax, will ya."

"Sorry. Sorry."

We walked in and, as Felix had told us to do, looked around for anyone who might know us. They were all strangers.

Cromie's was a vintage drugstore complete with soda fountain and windmill fans hanging from the ceiling. Even though it was a cool May day outside, the inside of Cromie's was muggy. The fans whirled frantically above us forcing me to almost shout to Lanner, who was standing right next to me.

"Okay Lanner," I said, "let's buy the candy bars."

The clerk behind the counter was a stocky, brutish-looking man with a square head covered by a crew cut. He was dressed in a smudgy white smock and he had pudgy meatball hands.

His mouth said nothing as he took our money for the candy bars. But his eyes were of the variety commonly worn by parents. They spoke plainly enough. "You are kids and therefore under suspicion. We will be watching you. Don't try anything."

Lanner bought two Snickers bars. I remember Lanner as being very big on Snickers. I bought a Hershey's chocolate and a Mounds bar. Then I remembered that a Mounds was a ten-cent candy bar. Since we figured this was going to be an expensive escapade into the erotic, I put the Mounds bar back and took another Hershey's.

After dropping our coins into the clerk's pudgy meatball hands, Lanner and I began unwrapping our candy bars as we pretended to head toward the door. At the last second, we nonchalantly veered right and headed straight for the paperback and magazine racks.

Although Felix the Filth Fiend Lindor had told us not to bother with the magazines, one of the covers was too tantalizing to ignore. "How Debbie Keeps Eddie Up ALL Night," the cover line read. I opened up the magazine and began looking for the article.

Lanner was already on his knees looking through

the paperbacks on the bottom rung of the rack. When he saw what I was doing, he shouted something up to me. I couldn't hear him the first time because of the noise from one of the whirling windmill fans, which was hanging directly over our heads. I yelled back at him to repeat it.

"I said," bellowed Lanner, "that I thought Felix told us to forget about the magazines and to concentrate on the paperbacks."

"Yeah, he did," I shouted back. "I just wanted to check out a few of them for myself." I could tell by Lanner's look that he was irritated by my breach of self-discipline.

When I got to the article on Debbie and Eddie, I discovered that Debbie kept Eddie up all night by calling him on the phone every half hour. What a rob. Felix was right. I went over to Lanner, who was still on his knees next to the bookrack.

"Find anything good, Tom?"

"Nope. All I can see are a few cookbooks and some Spanish-English dictionaries."

I began searching out the books that were buried behind the others, figuring that maybe Cromie made it a point of hiding the dirty books so that only the people who wanted dirty books would know that Cromie was dirty enough to carry them. That's what I would have done if I owned a drugstore and sold dirty books. I wouldn't want the whole world to know I was selling dirty books. Just the people who wanted them. Of course, if I owned a drugstore, I wouldn't sell dirty books because it's a very dirty thing to do. There's a big difference between buying dirty books and selling dirty books.

Lanner and I were both flipping through the pages of different books, frantically searching for some fragments of filth. We were trying all the techniques Felix had taught us: selecting random samples from the beginning, middle, and ends of books, letting them fall open naturally in our hands, avoiding books that had the author's picture on the cover. Still nothing.

Lanner was getting nervous. He kept looking at either the Coca-Cola clock that was above the greeting card display or over at the clerk who was behind the counter.

Finally, Lanner said, "Hey, Eddie, let's get going. That clerk is beginning to look over here a lot."

"You go over and buy another candy bar," I said. "That'll keep him busy so I can keep looking. If I can't find anything by the time you get back here, we'll give up."

"Well, okay. But as soon as I buy the candy bar and get back here, we leave, right?"

"Right, Tom."

Lanner started for the counter, which was on the other side of the store.

I spotted it behind three other books. A thin, plain red-covered book with its title in gold letters: SANDRA THE SEX KITTEN, HOT FROM CINCINNATI. I didn't even bother opening it. I knew. This was the real thing.

Lanner was already on his way back from the counter with the Snickers bar in his hand.

"Hey, Tom," I yelled, "I found one."

He didn't hear me, even though he was only ten feet away, because of the loud whirring of the windmill fans dangling from the ceiling. So I said it again, only much louder. But just as I started, the engines on the fans stopped and I heard a voice shout through Cromie's Drugstore.

"Hey, Tom, I found a great dirty book."

Everyone in the store turned around and stared at me and SANDRA THE SEX KITTEN, HOT FROM CINCINNATI, which was now burning in my hand.

Tom stopped for a second, stunned by the voice,

and then continued on toward the door, walking by as if he didn't know me.

I tried to reach behind my back and replace SANDRA THE SEX KITTEN, HOT FROM CINCINNATI back on the rack without being obvious. I heard it slap to the floor. I picked it up and jammed it back on the rack. As I turned around, I saw the crew-cut, square head behind the counter point a finger of his pudgy meatball fist at me.

"Hey, kid, get."

I got.

Lanner was waiting for me about a block away.

"You rat, Lanner, deserting me like that."

"What could I have done? I bet that guy behind the counter threw you out and you didn't get the book anyway."

"Well, it's pretty obvious that I didn't get the book, Lanner. Where the hell could I be hiding it? In my ear?"

"You got thrown out, didn't you."

We began walking toward the bus stop a block away.

"What are you going to tell Felix and Hellger?" Lanner asked.

"I don't know. But no matter what we tell them, we're gonna be lucky if Felix ever lets us back in the cave again."

The double-feature show was within a few minutes of ending when Lanner and I got to the bus stop in front of the Hollywood Theater. I was hoping a bus would come along before the crowd got out. It's very depressing to sit on a sunny Saturday afternoon bus and listen to a bunch of kids talk about a double feature you haven't seen, especially when the reason that you haven't seen it is because you're so stupid.

As I stared down Seventy-ninth Street, searching for a bus, I noticed Lanner looking at the glossy glass-enclosed pictures of the double feature, which hung gleaming on the front of the Hollywood Theater.

"Come on, Lanner, forget it."

"Yeah," he said, "I'll be right there." But he just kept standing there in front of the glass-enclosed pictures, awkwardly shifting his weight from one foot to the other, his hands punched deep into his pants pockets.

I looked up at the massive face of the Hollywood Theater with its marquee teeth and back down at Lanner, who was standing directly under the marquee. I imagined the Hollywood Theater's tongue rising out of the sidewalk and casually flipping Lanner through the door, gulping him down into oblivion. An amusing thought except that the Hollywood Theater was the kind of building that, if it could have done such a thing, would have.

I've always had a problem with buildings intimidating me. Not all of them. Just some. I can walk up to most buildings, jerk open their doors, and rumble through their bods with no trouble at all. They're dirt under my feet and they know it. With other buildings, it's more of a standoff.

There have been a few brick bullies that, no matter how many times I have entered them, look upon my presence as a degradation of their dignity. The Hollywood Theater was one of those.

I was six years old when I first entered the Hollywood Theater. It was on a Saturday afternoon, of course. Immediately, I realized that I was out of my league. As I walked past her massive glass-frame doors and under her multicolored embroidered ceiling, I felt my body slowly shrinking. By the time I got to the candy counter, I was less than three inches tall. The same thing happened every time I walked inside of her.

The lobby of the Hollywood Theater was about a mile long and a city block wide. If you passed through the door marked Aisle 1, you found yourself in the actual seating arena, which was surrounded by a Roman courtyard, complete with columns, windowed walls, and a real staircase that wound its way up into a cube of black.

A couple of times when the show was over, I'd try to sneak up those stairs to see what was up there. Each time, I'd get caught by the same little fat usher with the falsetto voice who kept his flashlight stuck in his belt in front of his belly. When he needed the flashlight, he'd simply turn it on and twist it around in his belt until it was pointing where he wanted it to. I was almost halfway up the stairs once when he caught me. I heard the squeaky voice, looked down, and saw the flashlight beaming at me from his navel.

"Hey, kid, get the hell out of there."

"Isn't this the way out?"

"I said, get the hell out of there."

"It's not, huh?"

It was always a clear night above the seats of the Hollywood Theater. Where the ceiling should have been was a black sky speckled with twinkling stars of all sizes. I thought they might have been lights stuck in the ceiling, but I really wasn't sure. Even today, there is still some doubt in my mind.

The washrooms of the Hollywood Theater had more class than my living room. And they were bigger. Rows of huge round sinks encased by marble counters. In the lobby of the washrooms was a triple mirror where I first discovered the back of my head. I used to stand in front of that triple mirror for fifteen minutes at a time, amazed at the sight of the back of my head.

For the first few years of grammar school, the only way I was allowed to go to the Hollywood Theater was if I went with my older sister. Her taste in movies was slop. Doris Day musicals and Lucille Ball stuff. I spent most of my time then looking up at the stars, taking walks in the lobby, or staring at the back of my head in the washroom. Sometimes I'd stand in front of the candy counter and watch the caramel corn being made.

The Hollywood Theater caramel corn was made in a large steel pot behind the popcorn counter by a pimply-faced, stringy-haired, flat-chested high school dropout who had chewed-up dirt under her fingernails. Her personality was no bargain, either. But she sure could make caramel corn.

She'd shovel some corn from a cardboard barrel into the steel pot. Then she'd open a large jar of caramel and hold it upside down over the steel pot. The caramel would slowly ooze out. GLOP GLOP GLOP. Sometimes it would take as long as five minutes for the caramel jar to empty out. It was at such times that the pimply-faced, stringy-haired, flat-chested high school dropout chose to display her Seventy-ninth Street vocabulary.

After the caramel was in the steel pot, she'd take her two forty-five-pound hands, wrap them around a wooden oar, and stir that pot of caramel and corn as smooth and fast as if it were empty. Her arms moved so frantically that her feet used to float a few inches off the floor. If there was a dull show running, she'd sometimes have as many kids in the lobby watching her as were inside watching the show.

After the stirring and twenty minutes to let it dry—caramel corn must dry you know—she'd start scooping it out with popcorn boxes, filling and flapping them closed, all performed in one easy, fluid motion. That girl had a great pair of hands. If she hadn't been a female, and so ugly besides, she would have made a great second baseman.

Within minutes, caramel-corn boxes would fill the counter. Two other fairly normal-looking girls, who also worked the popcorn counter, did the actual selling. The supply of caramel corn would be quickly depleted and the pimply-faced, stringy-haired, flat-chested high school dropout would once again start the steel-pot procedure.

Like all great caramel corn, a box of the Hollywood Theater's caramel corn could never be completely consumed. The first fistful would be ecstatic. The second, delicious. The third, fair. Then you'd feel that blob of caramel corn swelling in your stomach and you'd know that one more gulp of it would ignite the blob and send it rocketing up through your throat, knocking your head off.

By the fifth grade, I was allowed to go to the Hollywood Theater without the moral support of my sister. Lanner was the guy I most enjoyed going to the show with, but he rarely had enough money. So I usually ended up going with Johnny Hellger.

He had a mind almost as dirty as Felix the Filth Fiend Lindor's except that whenever Felix talked about sex he would do it in a normal tone of voice while Johnny Hellger's voice always dropped to an almost inaudible whisper, interspersed with a lot of low-throated chuckles. Although Johnny Hellger's mind wasn't quite as filthy as Felix's, it was certainly a lot moldier.

Johnny Hellger always had to get a receipt from the cashier to prove to his mother that he had in fact gone to the Hollywood Theater instead of to the Cosmo Theater across the street. Johnny Hellger's mother, like mine, was a firm follower of the Catholic Legion of Decency ratings. The Hollywood showed only A-1 pictures. The Cosmo wasn't as inhibited.

A few times, Johnny Hellger had managed to slip over there and catch some A-III and B movies. He claimed he saw a C (for condemned) movie once. Johnny Hellger tried to tell me about it but I wouldn't listen. You can go to Hell for just hearing about a C movie.

Once Johnny Hellger had gotten past the cashier, he would head up the stairs that led to the balcony. You had to be fourteen years old or older to sit up there. Although Johnny Hellger was only ten years old, he seemed to look at least twenty years older every time he stepped into the Hollywood Theater. I had to be contented with the first-floor routine.

Besides being closer to the stars up there, Johnny Hellger could also get his cheap thrills watching the high school kids make out. During intermission, he'd meet me in the lobby. There, over a package of M&M's, Johnny Hellger would tell me, in an almost inaudible whisper spiced with low-voiced chuckles, the sex scenes he had witnessed.

"Come on, Lanner," I yelled, "there's a bus coming." Lanner took one last look at a glass-enclosed picture that featured a scene from *Savage Sundown*, turned, and reluctantly began shuffling toward me. Too late. The Saturday afternoon double feature had apparently ended. Already, kids were beginning to explode out of the doors of the Hollywood Theater.

I knew how they felt. If the two movies were good, you'd sit through four hours of almost total darkness, the only light coming from the stars overhead and a few exit signs that you could see speckled along the edges of the dark. You'd sit there so long you'd actually forget that it wasn't nighttime.

After the show, you'd walk through the lobby feeling tired and lousy, like you'd been in school all day. It wasn't until you made the turn around the popcorn machine and saw the daylight through the front doors that you realized it was light out. Like finding a few hours of sunshine you'd thought you'd already lived through. It felt good to discover that sunlight and it really excited you. That's why people exploded out of the Hollywood Theater instead of just walking out.

The bus ride home was a classic. A real classic. All these kids around Lanner and me talking about two movies that neither of us had seen. They talked about different scenes, why they thought the Range Rider left the girl behind at the ranch before going into town. How Driman, the crooked bank owner who was secretly the leader of the gang, got killed. And how the ending was so terrific. Stuff like that. It was very depressing.

Two kids, sitting behind Lanner and me, were eating Hollywood Theater caramel corn. The sounds of their caramel corn crackled in my ear lobes, slid down through my inner ear, and right into my mouth. And all I had to chew on were my cheeks.

The Saturday afternoon had diluted into dusk by the time the bus reached Seven Holy Tombs and our block. Hopping off the bus and heading home.

"Wanna get together tomorrow after mass and play some baseball?" I asked.

"Can't. Gotta do work around the house tomorrow. Did you think of something to say to Felix in the cave after school Monday?"

"No, I haven't. Have you?"

"No."

We were standing in front of Lanner's house now.

"Well," said Lanner, "I'd better get in, dinner's probably on the table."

"Yeah, see you later."

I started trotting down the street. I didn't want to be late, either. My mother made a big deal out of Saturday night suppers. I began thinking about the whole afternoon. Cromie's Drugstore, SANDRA THE SEX KITTEN, HOT FROM CINCINNATI, and how I'd never know the ecstasy contained between her covers. The Hollywood Theater and how I'd never again get a chance to see those two movies. I thought about having to meet Felix in the dirt-hill cave on Monday after school with the story of my failure.

I slowed down my trotting to a walk. Sometimes you just don't feel like running to get where you're going.

"Yo, Eddie." It was 3:30, Monday afternoon and I was changing into my after-school clothes when I heard Lanner calling for me at the side door of my house. In my neighborhood, no kid ever knocked on the door for you. He simply stood at the side door and shouted, "Yo . . ." whatever your name was.

On the way over to the dirt-hill cave, Lanner and I tried to decide on a story to tell Felix. We tested and rejected numerous accounts. In desperation, we agreed to tell Felix the truth. Neither of us felt comfortable with it, but it seemed like the only thing to do. We were walking so slowly that we were a half hour late by the time we got to the prairie.

Lanner and I squiggled through the high weeds, which had by now totally eclipsed the dirt-hill cave from street view. We were only a few feet away from the cave, but were still among the weeds when we saw him standing just outside the cave entrance: that brutish-looking man with the pudgy meatball hands and the square head covered by the crew cut. The clerk from Cromie's Drugstore.

He was listening intently to the conversation going on inside the cave but Lanner and I were too far away to hear what either Felix or Johnny Hellger was saying.

Suddenly the clerk from Cromie's Drugstore became enraged at something he apparently overheard. He stooped down and stuck his arm into the entrance of the cave, yelling for whoever was in there to come out.

Johnny Hellger came running out, barely avoiding

the grasp of the man, and ran into the weeds, heading straight for us. Felix the Filth Fiend wasn't so lucky. As he came out of the dirt-hill cave, the clerk from Cromie's Drugstore snared him by the arm and started dragging him toward a blue sedan that was parked in an alley behind the prairie.

"Oh my God!" yelled Lanner, "the cave's being raided."

Lanner and I grabbed Johnny Hellger as he started to run past us through the weeds. At first, not realizing who had grabbed him, his body flinched statically from our touch. Then Johnny Hellger saw who it was.

"Let go of me you guys," he said. "I gotta get the hell out of here."

"Don't you know who that guy is?" I asked. "We gotta help Felix."

Johnny Hellger ripped away from Lanner and me, and began once again to skitter through the weeds. He yelled back at us.

"You're goddamn right I know who he is. And I'm not going back to help Felix. I've never seen old man Lindor so mad."

XI *Blah on the Altar Boys*

Deborah came to St. Bastion's fifth grade in October. She was a transfer student. The nun put her in the double seat next to me. Deborah was pure class. She wore rings on her fingers, her dress came to only an inch below her knees, and she had a terrific build on the days that she wore it.

As soon as Deborah would finish her English workbook assignment, she'd take a green hard-covered book out of her desk. On its cover was a young couple holding hands while walking by some tall, overhanging trees. Deborah would often read the same page two or three times.

Once I asked her what the book was about. "It's about love," she sighed. "About love." Man, the way she said it, that word "love" just hung between us right through spelling period.

A few weeks after she arrived, Deborah caught me in the most embarrassing situation possible: she saw me with my parents. Our family had gone out to buy some shoes and we were walking back to our car, which was parked about a block away from the store, when Deborah and a few of her girl friends walked by. She smiled and said hello. I mumbled something back. My father grinned and started teasing me about having a girl friend. He was weird that way. Deborah actually saw me with my parents. I felt like a real jerk.

For the first few weeks, I tried engaging Deborah in some casual conversation. But it was no go. I'd do all the talking and she wouldn't do any of the listening. It was almost unnatural. People in double seats always talked to one another. Sharing double seats was almost like being related.

I asked Depki to find out what the trouble was. Talking to Deborah, he quickly discovered the problem.

"She thinks you're a very nice guy, but that's about it," said Depki.

"What does that mean?" I asked.

"It means she thinks you're blah."

"Blah?"

"Blah," Depki repeated emphatically. "You gotta realize, Ryan," he said, "that there are two kinds of kids in this school—those who are 'in' and those who are 'out.' The kids who are 'in' are the ones who get noticed by everybody else. Now to get noticed, you usually gotta be real good at something, like say sports, or say you're real smart in school. Or you're really stupid. Real stupid kids get noticed, too. You gotta be something really different, you know."

"Where did you learn all this?" I asked.

"From my older brother," said Depki. "He knows all kinds of things about what it takes for somebody to be a hotshot. When he was telling me about this stuff, he says to me, 'Mike, what do you notice about a train when you're standing up at 103rd and Langlen waitin' for it to go by?' And I says, 'I don't know. The whole train, I guess.' My older brother says, 'No you don't, Mike. The only thing you remember about that train is the engine and the caboose. All the regular cars just rumble by without you ever really seeing them. That's the way life is too, Mike,' says my brother. 'If you wanna be a hotshot, you gotta be either an engine or a caboose.'

"Another thing my older brother told me," said Depki, "is that 'in' people don't mix with 'out' people very much."

Depki didn't have to say any more. We both knew. I didn't cut it. I was brilliantly blah in everything I did.

Not Deborah. She was probably the greatest volleyball player in the history of the St. Bastion volleyball team. She had a fantastic personality, too. Everyone liked her except for a few girls who were jealous of her. And brains? I can't think of a page in her workbook that wasn't done.

One afternoon, right before dismissal, we were handing in our arithmetic homework. Actually, I never handed in any arithmetic homework in fifth grade. What I did was hand in all my fourth-grade arithmetic papers that I had left over from the previous year. They all look pretty much the same. The first time I tried it, I had the day's homework done so if the nun noticed my fourth-grade paper, I could just claim that I had accidentally handed in the wrong paper. But she didn't notice. So every day after that, I'd hand in a fourth-grade arithmetic paper. I guess the nun didn't check them because she never did catch on. The kid who came down the row to collect them never noticed the difference either. I was very proud of myself, outmaneuvering a nun.

Anyway, that afternoon, right after handing in my arithmetic homework, I whispered to Lanner, who sat four desks behind me, "Want to goof around together after school?"

"Naw," said Lanner, "I can't. Got to go over to church."

"Church? On a Tuesday afternoon?"

"Yeah, Father Durkin's holding a meeting for all the fifth-grade boys who want to become altar boys. Didn't you hear Sister announce that this morning?"

"Yeah, sure I did," I said. "But why do you want to become an altar boy?"

Lanner laughed. "Gee, I don't know. I just think I'd like it. Why don't you come along with me?"

"I don't think so, Tom. I'd like to, but I gotta goof around this afternoon." And then I heard voices in my head.

"You mean, Deborah, that you sit in a double seat with Eddie Ryan! Why, he's the greatest altar boy in the entire school. The greatest!"

Lanner was getting his books ready to go home.

"Hey, Lanner," I whispered, "I'll go with you." The nun had spotted me.

"Mr. Ryan, were you talking? Come up here to the front of the room."

Later that day, as I contemplated the life of an altar boy, I thought to myself that perhaps this was the opportunity that God was waiting for to single me out as someone special. Naturally, I was quite familiar with the stories about God appearing to different saints. Quite a few of them were children, like the kid at Lourdes and the three kids who were involved with "Our Lady of Fatima." Not that I thought I was a saint. But I bet a lot of those people might not have been saints either until God appeared to them. And what better time was there for God to appear to me than when I was running around as an altar boy. I knew there wasn't much possibility of such a thing happening but that didn't stop me from thinking about it. Sort of like a Catholic's dream of making it big in Hollywood.

Becoming an altar boy was easy enough. All you had to do was memorize some Latin and know how to move around the altar. I didn't even bother learning the Latin. I'd just put my head down and mumble nonsense syllables. A lot of the other altar boys did that, too, I think.

But getting to be known around school as the best altar boy at St. Bastion's wasn't going to be as easy as I had planned. I had figured that a lot of other blah guys like myself would be joining the altar boys, looking for their place in the sun, and I was right about that. But according to most of the pew population, Bobby Bracken had just about claimed the title of the greatest altar boy at St. Bastion's, a title left vacant by the graduation of Sam "The Saint" Simpson, who had insisted that Christ had made numerous appearances to him in the coatroom.

There is a Bobby Bracken in every parish. The kid who seems to hold all patent rights on piety. Before he is even out of the womb, his mother is telling him, and all of her friends, that he is going into the priesthood. The nuns adore him, the parish priests patronize him, and his father doesn't know him. He's the kid who tells anyone who will listen that he is going to become a priest and never even considers being a policeman. The worst part is that he usually does become a priest.

Years later, Bobby Bracken would, in his sophomore year, be thrown out of St. Philip's Seminary after being caught in an empty classroom "saying mass" while using sugar wafers for Holy Communion. From there, Bobby Bracken would move on to a notorious career in homosexuality. But in the fifth grade, he was still a formidable power.

The sure sign of being a great altar boy was getting a lot of wedding assignments from Father Durkin, who was in charge of the altar boys. It was customary for the bridegroom to tip the altar boys a few bucks for their efforts. Thus, an altar boy, like most professionals, was judged not by his actual performance but by the size of his bankroll.

According to Father Durkin, the reason that Bobby Bracken got so many weddings to serve was because Bobby Bracken was constantly filling in for guys who failed to show up for their assignments. For instance, if an altar boy didn't show up for one of the daily masses, say the six o'clock mass, Father Durkin claimed he would call up Bobby Bracken, who would come over to church and take the absent kid's place.

Bobby Bracken was supposedly called because he lived only a half a block from church. A lot of kids lived just as close to church as Bobby Bracken, but none of them were ever called. I doubt if Bobby Bracken was ever called that much, either. I think Father Durkin just said that. Maybe Bobby Bracken was called once or twice, but that was about it.

"The reason," said Depki, who quit the altar boys after a week, "that Bobby Bracken gets all those weddings is because he's a sticky sweet sonofabitch who's constantly going around telling everyone how he's going to be a missionary in Africa and that dummy

Father Durkin eats up that kind of shit." I think Depki was right.

Lanner and I, who were usually assigned to serve together, had had only one wedding by the end of November. Right in the middle of the ceremony, I somehow managed to drop the tray with the wedding bands on it. All over the church, you could hear them bonking along the floor. We didn't make any money on that one.

Next in importance to the weddings was the children's eight o'clock mass in the basement church, because of the prestige of performing in front of the entire school. Father Durkin was fair about that. He assigned different kids each week to serve it so that all of us got our chance to be holy hotshots in front of the student body. At one of the weekly Monday afternoon altar-boy meetings, Father Durkin announced that on the following Sunday, the children's eight o'clock mass would be served by Bobby Bracken, Tom Lanner, and myself. It was the only mass that I know, for a fact, God did not attend.

I went to bed early that Saturday night. At that age, I still believed all the garbage people told me about having to have a lot of rest if I wanted to do something well. Of course since then, I've discovered that the exact opposite is true, having enjoyed some of my greatest days while being virtually totally asleep.

That night, I dreamed of Deborah. She was so impressed with the way I served the eight o'clock mass that she bragged me to her girl friends all the way home from church. The following Monday morning, she stared at me constantly as we sat in our double seats, and laughed hysterically at anything I said. I asked the nun if I could go back to the coatroom to get a pen that I had left in my jacket pocket, I looked up and saw Deborah standing a few feet away from me. Deborah and I, alone in the coatroom, her lips gently floated into a gentle smile, her arms began extending toward me. . . .

I abruptly awoke to the clattering of ice chips bouncing off my bedroom window. For a split second, I vainly hoped that this was a dream and that the reality was Deborah and I in the coatroom. But the clattering of the ice chips continued.

I pulled up the window shade and saw the early morning sky retching rain and snow. Everything below the window, tree branches, sidewalks, cars, was glossy with ice. As I climbed out of bed, I realized that I had a headache and my stomach hurt. My mouth felt like I hadn't brushed my teeth in eight years. If it hadn't been a Sunday, I would have thought it was a report-card day. My mouth always felt like I hadn't brushed my teeth in eight years on report-card days.

A few minutes later, my legs moving in robot fashion, I inched across the icy sidewalk toward St. Bastion Church. Ankles remained rigid as each foot slowly plopped down. The body, constantly wary of the foot losing its grip, would cautiously shift its weight onto it. Once secure, the body would swing out the other foot and the procedure would repeat itself. My eyes were concentrating so intently on this plodding procession of my feet that my unguided head ran straight into a wall of St. Bastion Church.

After going down the basement steps and into the church sacristy, I went into the altar boys' closet and tried to find a cassock my size. There weren't any. The nuns, who each Saturday night took half the cassocks over to the convent to be cleaned, had apparently managed to grab all the cassocks that were even near my size. The closest I could get was one cassock that came to an inch above my knees and another that ended two feet beyond my shoes. I put on the one that was two feet too long. Father Durkin would give you a very hard time if you tried to wear a cassock that was too short.

As I finished buttoning it, I stood in front of the full-length mirror that hung on the back door of the closet. The cassock had swallowed me whole. I was afraid that when Deborah saw me in that cassock, she was going to think she was sharing her double seat with a dwarf.

Lanner came walking into the sacristy. He looked at my cassock, the bottom of which lay in folds around my feet.

"Say, Ryan, did you take a bath last night? You look like you've shrunk."

"That's very funny, Lanner. But I'm afraid that you're not going to be quite so amused when you look in the closet and discover that you're going to have to wear the same thing." Lanner was about the same size that I was.

He started looking around at the different cassocks in the closet. "Where are all the normal-size ones? There's nothing here but longs and shorts." Lanner started putting on a cassock even longer than mine.

"I don't know," I said. "All I know is I'm having trouble keeping my hands free with these crazy sleeves drooping over them."

Just then, Bobby Bracken glided into the sacristy, a cassock, encased in a plastic cleaning bag, slung over his shoulder.

"Good morning, fellas! Say, what's with the long cassocks?"

"Where did you get that cassock, Bracken?" I demanded.

"Oh, this is my own cassock."

"Your own cassock?"

"That's right. Father Durkin told me that since I was serving so many masses I should have my own cassock. This way, my mother can keep it nice and clean and it won't get dirty by hanging in the closet with all the other cassocks."

Lanner muttered something about how this mass might turn into a funeral mass but Bobby Bracken didn't seem to hear him.

"Hey, Ryan, which one of us is going to sit on the side?" Bobby Bracken asked me as he was putting on his cassock.

It took only two altar boys to serve a mass. But Father Durkin had to assign three altar boys to each Sunday mass because so many people attended mass on Sunday. At Communion time, a couple of priests would have to come over from the rectory and help out the priest who was saying the mass serve Holy Communion. Each priest needed an altar boy to assist him.

As the priest would place a host of the Holy Communion on the tongue of the communicant, the altar boy would hold a paten, a metal disk with a handle attached, under the chin of the recipient. This was done, not so much because of the danger of the host, or the Eucharist as it is also called, falling off the person's tongue, although that possibility existed, but because microscopic crumbs of the host supposedly fell from the priest's fingers when he handled it. Since Catholics believe that the Holy Eucharist is the actual body and blood of Christ, it's vital that no part of it ever hit the floor. After the Communion part of the mass, the priest would wipe the paten off into the chalice, the gold cup where the Holy Eucharist was kept.

So although three altar boys were needed for a Sunday mass, only two of them actually served it. The third altar boy knelt at a kneeler, which was to one side of the altar, until Communion time when he was needed to help one of the priests serve Holy Communion.

As I said before, Depki was right about Bobby

Bracken. Bobby Bracken was what being a sonofabitch is all about. He always went around telling people how he couldn't wait to become a missionary and start saving souls for Christ. And how if he was real lucky he might get a chance to become a martyr for Christ.

All of us, during our more pious moments, thought stuff like that. But we didn't go around telling everybody mainly because we knew, once we'd gotten out of the mood, we'd regret that we had shot off our mouths.

Not Bobby Bracken. He was a real weirdo. I met his mother a few times and she was even weirder than Bobby. It was probably her fault that her kid was so strange. Or maybe it was the other way around.

Bobby Bracken was very friendly toward everyone. I have to admit that. I'm not saying he was not a royal pain in the ass. He was. And he probably figured that being nice to people was part of the game when you were planning on becoming a missionary for Christ. Still, he was pretty nice toward people. So when he asked me which guy was going to sit on the side, I didn't feel like telling him that Lanner and I wanted to serve the mass and have him sit it out. Of course, I knew that if I could convince Bobby Bracken to sit on the side, it would look to a lot of the kids like Lanner and I were better servers than Bobby Bracken since we were serving the mass and he wasn't.

"What do you feel like doing, Bobby?" I asked.

"I feel like serving this morning," said Bobby Bracken, the tips of his phony smile almost touching his ear lobes.

"I'll sit on the side," said Lanner.

"You don't have to do that, Tom," I said. "Why don't we all flip coins and the odd man sits out."

But as soon as Bobby Bracken heard Lanner's

words, he started heading down the narrow passageway that ran behind the altar and over to the priests' sacristy, leaving Lanner and I alone.

"Look, Tom," I said, "you don't have to take that kind of stuff from Bracken. We'll just tell him we're going to serve the mass and that'll be it. He won't be able to do anything about it. We probably won't get the chance to serve this eight o'clock mass again for the rest of the year. Bracken gets it a couple of times a month."

I didn't really think Bobby Bracken got the eight o'clock mass that much but that's what I told Lanner.

"That's okay, Eddie. I don't feel like serving today, anyway. You serve it with Bobby. I'd just as soon sit on the side. I got up this morning feeling kind of sick."

"Yeah, so did I, Tom. It must be the weather or something."

Lanner walked over to the sacristy window and looked out at the swirling, icy snow. You could still hear it clattering against the window. "Boy, it sure is lousy outside," he said.

"Come on, Tom, let's get over to the priests' sacristy."

"You go on, Eddie. I'm gonna stand here and look out the window for a few minutes."

When I got over to the priests' sacristy, Father Durkin was putting on his vestments, assisted by Bobby Bracken, of course.

"Good morning, Father."

"Good morning, uh . . ."

"Ryan, Father."

"That's right. Of course. Ryan, Ryan," he mumbled.

Father Durkin was putting on the last of his vestments. "Where's the other altar boy?" he asked.

"Here he comes now, Father," I said. Lanner was just emerging from the passageway.

"Good morning, Father," Lanner said.

"Good morning, uh . . ."

"Lanner, Father."

"That's right. Lanner, Lanner," Father Durkin mumbled.

The St. Bastion bells, dangling in the tiny tower atop the church, began counting out the hour in their low, monotonous groan as the four of us slowly swished out onto the altar. Without actually tilting my head from its straight-on stare, all great altar boys constantly stare straight on, I managed to sneak a glance over at the girls' side of the church.

There was Deborah, in the third row, looking very surprised that it was I, her own double-seat partner, who was serving the eight o'clock mass. I was determined that I was going to turn this ordinary children's eight o'clock basement mass into a brilliant performance. One that would have the entire school talking about it. And Deborah would casually mention to her volleyball teammates, "My double-seat partner is Eddie Ryan, you know. The best altar boy in St. Bastion's."

Bobby Bracken and I genuflected together at the base of the steps, in the center of the altar, and turned our backs on one another as we moved to our respective positions, the opposite corners of the first altar step.

I was within a foot of my position when I felt a tug. I tried taking a step, but it was no go. I looked over my shoulder and saw Bobby Bracken standing a few feet behind me and staring up at the altar as if he was in a trance or something. He was standing on the bottom of my oversized cassock. Still facing the other way, I tried whispering to him.

"Bracken, will you get off my cassock." I tried moving forward again. He was still on it. I gave a tug on the cassock. No reaction. A harder tug. Again no reaction. I had no choice. I turned around and walked up to Bobby Bracken, who still appeared as if he was in some kind of a trance, just staring up at the altar.

"Bracken, you're standing on my cassock."

His head slowly turned and gazed at me, his eyes glazed even more than usual. He suddenly seemed to snap out of it. "Oh," he said mechanically as he calmly removed his feet from the bottom of my cassock.

"Thanks a lot," I whispered. I nodded my head sarcastically and tried to sound sarcastic, too. But that's very hard to do when you're whispering.

I began heading back toward my position at the corner of the bottom altar step, head bowed, my eyes fixed on my feet. All humble people go around with their heads bowed. In order to be a great altar boy, one must be humble.

My bow-bent head bumped into something. It was Father Durkin coming down the altar steps to begin the prayers at the foot of the altar.

"What are you doing? Uh . . . uh . . . Ryan, isn't it?"

"Sorry, Father." I quickly stepped around him.

Five minutes later, when I had to move the missal from one side of the altar to the other, the book stand collapsed. Bobby Bracken was delighted. Being a future missionary of Christ, he refused to outwardly show it, but I could tell anyway.

In a certain part of the mass, the altar boy rings a small bell three times, very loudly. Each time the bell is rung, everyone in the church bows his head and thumps his chest with his fist. The reasons for all of this are very complicated and you probably wouldn't believe them even if I told you. But that's the way it is. The signal for the altar boy to ring the bell is when the priest puts his hands, palms down, out over the chalice.

I was grinding my teeth, thinking about the bookstand collapse, when Bobby Bracken whispered to me.

"Hey, Ryan! . . . Ryan!"

Regaining consciousness, I looked up and thought I saw Father Durkin's hands over the chalice. I grabbed the little bell from the step in front of me and began frantically shaking it.

The sound of fists pounding into chests could be heard throughout the church. THUMP THUMP THUMP THUMP THUMP THUMP. I rang the bell a second time. There were thumps, but not as many as the first time. The third time, I heard only one thump and that was my own.

Father Durkin looked over his shoulder at me from the top of the altar, started to say something, and then just slowly shook his head and went back to what he was doing. "Nice going, Ryan," Bobby Bracken whispered, "you just rang the bell five minutes ahead of time."

"What were you whispering at me for, then?"

"I was trying to tell you that you've got your cassock on inside out."

I felt for the label behind my neck. It was on the outside. Bobby Bracken was saying something else but I didn't hear him. I was no longer thinking of how I was going to impress the whole school or fascinate Deborah with my holy moves. My mind held but one thought, survival.

Praying to God to turn me into a turtle, I pulled my head down as deep as I could into my oversized cassock. It was dark and warm inside my shell and no world existed outside of it. But still I heard the bell ringing and the thump thump thumps.

One knocked-down candle and dropped paten later, the mass was over. My only consolation was that the mass moved from a one-ring circus to a three-ring circus. During Communion time, Bobby Bracken got careless with the paten and chopped it into some kid's Adam's apple. The kid almost strangled to death right at the Communion rail. Lanner got caught in a rundown.

Father Durkin believed that in order for one to be close to God and a good altar boy, one had to move slowly while on the altar. So we altar boys had to walk with baby steps whenever Father Durkin was around. Father Boyle, however, who was one of the priests who came over from the rectory to help hand out Communion, believed in speed. Especially on Sunday mornings when he was in a big rush to get the mass over with so he could talk and goof around with the parishioners as they came out of the church.

Father Boyle was working out of one of the side altars, which was around the corner from the main altar. Lanner, who had to go over to the side altar to assist Father Boyle in serving Communion, had to crawl until he got to the corner and then, once he was out of sight of Father Durkin and in view of Father Boyle, had to almost run across the altar, spurred on by Father Boyle's encouraging whispers. "Come on, will ya. We haven't got all day, you know."

Lanner spent the entire Communion time either sprinting or braking, depending on who was watching him. To the kids in the pews, Lanner probably looked like he was going crazy.

After mass, when we had gotten back into the priests' sacristy, Father Durkin had things to say.

"Look at you two guys," Father Durkin said to Lanner and me. Bobby Bracken was quietly putting Father's vestments away. The bastard. "How you two guys managed to become altar boys, I don't know. Look at you. Your cassocks are three feet too long and Ryan, you even have yours on backward.

Lanner, I've never seen an altar boy handle himself as poorly as you."

Lanner. I couldn't believe it. Father Durkin was going after Lanner. I had damn near single-handedly brought down a two-thousand-year-old institution and Father Durkin was going after Lanner.

"I want a twenty-five-hundred-word essay from you by next Friday on how to be a good altar boy, Lanner," said Father Durkin. "Either do the essay or quit the altar boys."

As the two of us turned and headed toward the altar boys' sacristy, we heard Father Durkin saying, "Nice mass, Bobby, nice mass."

"That Durkin's crazy," I said to Lanner as we took off our cassocks in the altar boys' closet. "Bobby Bracken goofed up the mass more than you did and I messed up ten times more than both of you guys put together."

"Don't worry about it, Eddie," Lanner said. "Durkin's an asshole, so what can you expect."

"You're not going to do the penalty, are you?"

"I don't know what I'm going to do yet," he said as he hung his three-feet-too-long cassock up on a closet hook.

The following Friday, Lanner handed in his twenty-five-hundred-word essay to Father Durkin and then quit the altar boys.

As I walked home from mass, the rain-speckled snow was still coming down. But now, instead of icing everything, it was simply self-destructing into slush. I thought about Lanner and the rotten deal he had gotten from Father Durkin. And I wondered why it always seemed to be Lanner who got rotten deals. I thought about Deborah, too. About how I'd be lucky now if she didn't ask the nun to change her seat. But I thought mostly about Lanner.

The next morning, I got into my double seat just

before the bell rang. Deborah was reading her green book with the lovers on the cover.

"Can I borrow a sheet of paper?" I asked. I had tons of paper. I just wanted to see if she'd even talk to me.

Deborah reached inside her desk. "Here, take five sheets. I have plenty. There's a volleyball game this afternoon, you know."

"Oh, there is?"

"Over at Crest Hill Park. I never see you at the games. How come you never go?"

"Oh, I'm pretty busy being an altar boy, you know."

"You! Why, you're the worst altar boy in the school. On the way home from mass yesterday, all my girl friends were saying how funny and cute you looked up there on the altar. Are you going to go to the volleyball game this afternoon?" The bell rang and we had to stand for prayers.

I don't remember praying, though. All I could see was a freight train rumbling by and everyone straining to see if the caboose was in sight yet.

XII Sister Edna

Sister Edna, my seventh-grade nun, was a huge woman with freckled hands. On her desk could be found the usual pile of garbage that nuns accumulate: corrected papers, grade books, paper clips, staples, and confiscated contraband.

In addition, Sister Edna also kept seven small plastic statues, one for each day of the week she said, and, in the upper right-hand corner of the desk, the only item that was never subjected to being moved or used: a twelve-hundred-page book of *Louis, King of France.* Even its bookmark, a Saint Joseph holy card, was immune to movement, always seemingly wedged between the same pages.

Whenever Sister Edna got mad, she'd make a gun out of her hand and wave the barrel finger right in your face as she bawled you out or just before she slugged you.

She was kind of an old nun, Sister Edna. Not real old, but kind of. I liked her. She didn't do a lot of terrifically kind things for me or any of that other Mr. Chips bullshit. There were over seventy kids in my seventh-grade classroom. Like any nun, Sister Edna spent most of her time just thinking up things for us to do. But she never went out of her way to make life miserable for anyone. For that reason alone, I liked her. She didn't make school fun. That would have been preposterous. But she did make it tolerable.

Sister Edna did do me a favor once, though. It was no big deal but it did give me an idea of what Sister Edna was all about. It was almost time for dismissal and she had given the class a few minutes to start on their English homework that was due the next day.

"Mr. Ryan, come up here to my desk." Sister Edna said it matter-of-factly so I wasn't too worried. I figured she wanted to see me about some routine paper work. I thought maybe I had forgotten to pay my milk money for that month.

"Wait out in the hall for me," Sister Edna said as I came up to her desk. I was shocked. Normally you heard the words "Wait out in the hall for me" only when you were about to receive such violent retribution for a previous escapade that it was going to be too gory for the rest of the class to witness.

As I walked toward the door, a few heads in the front row bobbed up from their work and grabbed a glance of me as I went by. Their faces had a tinge of sympathy diluted by a lot of self-satisfaction. Something like that gave everyone, with the exception of the kid who had to go out in the hall, a bright new outlook on life. "Things could be a lot worse," they'd tell themselves. "I could have been the guy out in the hall today."

As I stood out in the hallway, the only thing that I could think of that I had done wrong recently was I had been chewing on my pencil eraser when Sister Edna had called me up to her desk. Hardly cause for violent retribution, even for a nun.

I didn't have much time to worry about it because I was in the hall only a few seconds when Sister Edna came out to me, closing the classroom door behind her.

"Do you brush your teeth?" she asked. It was not the type of question I was expecting. Besides, even then, I realized it was a very personal one. But Sister Edna didn't ask me in a sarcastic tone of voice, as if she already knew the answer and just wanted to see if I'd lie. She asked like she really wanted to know. So I told her.

"Yes, Str. I brush them every morning." That wasn't exactly true. I didn't brush my teeth every morning. But I did brush them four or five times a week.

"Well, Eddie," Sister Edna said, "your breath is bad. It doesn't smell very good at all. It would help, I think, if you could brush harder and more often."

"Yes, Str, I will."

"Fine. Fine." Sister Edna opened the classroom door and went back to her desk and I went back to my seat. Heads popped up as Sister Edna and I came back into the room, disappointed, for they had heard no sounds of violence volume from the hallway.

It was no big deal. I wasn't embarrassed having Sister Edna tell me I had bad breath. That room was loaded with kids who had bad breath. Actually, I thought it was really nice that Sister Edna had even bothered to tell me. She didn't have to. I wasn't breathing around her all the time. She could have let me go through life with bad breath. What did it matter to her?

Most nuns wouldn't have bothered to tell me. Or if they had, they would have done it in front of the entire class and in a demeaning way, as if to say, "Hey, slob, have you got bad breath! Yech!"

But Sister Edna pointed it out to me as if she were telling me about an untied shoe. No moral connotation. She simply told me I had it and suggested a remedy to cure it. It was very unusual for anyone, especially a nun, to notice something wrong with you and not presume it was your fault. Very unusual.

By some divine decree, Lanner and I shared the same double seat for the entire seventh-grade year in Sister Edna's room. It was an unheard-of phenomenon at St. Bastion school that two good friends would end up sharing the same double seat. The nuns kept close track of who hung around with who and made it a point to keep at least four rows between good friends. But that year, their surveillance system slipped up and there in the seventh grade sat Lanner and I, together in a double seat.

I have always felt that it is the moral obligation of an occupant of a double seat to entertain and be entertained by his partner. Lanner totally agreed with my philosophy. We both considered ourselves superb exponents of the one-liner and it was during history period, when Sister Edna asked the class questions, that our hackneyed humor reached its heights.

For instance, Sister Edna would call on some kid and ask him in what year Lincoln was shot. While the kid was standing up and "uuhhhing," Lanner would point at his ear and whisper to me, "The left ear."

Stuff like that killed me. I whispered equally inane comments to him.

They don't seem very funny now. They wouldn't have seemed very funny then if they had been told anywhere but in the classroom. But I'm the sort of person who's most easily provoked into laughter when he's in a place where he has no business even smiling. A joke that would bore me on a street corner would break me up in a library. Lanner was that kind of jerk, too.

It was during these seventh-grade history periods that I developed an art that was to serve me well, not only in school, but as the years passed, through hundreds of hours of funerals, dull parties, and after-dinner speeches: the silent laugh.

At St. Bastion school, even smiling was suspect. Only troublemakers and kids who were enjoying themselves smiled. And at St. Bastion school, the only kids who enjoyed themselves *were* the troublemakers. So for those interested in self-preservation, smiling, much less actual laughing, was strictly out.

Normally, a laugh starts jelling in the stomach, springs through the throat, and ha's out the mouth. Like most things that shoot out the mouth, a laugh comes on an exhale. It's impossible, for instance, to talk and be breathing in at the same time.

The secret of the silent laugh is that just as the laugh is springing through the throat, you cut off your exhale stroke. The stomach vibrates slightly. Faint pitting sounds emit from the throat, but that's about it. In extreme cases, a great one-liner, well-timed, may cause the eyes to water and the stomach to experience minor muscle spasms. But even if a nun was looking right at you, the worse she could think was that you were going through a mild seizure of the dry heaves.

Unfortunately, Tom Lanner never mastered the silent laugh. His laughter always fell out in lopsided chunks. He was often caught, although even I was nabbed a few times.

Whether it was Lanner or I, or anyone else for that matter, who was detected, the procedure was the same. Sister Edna would call the culprit up to the front of the room.

"Were you talking?"

"Yes, Str."

Wham!

Sister Edna ran a very pleasant room. If you got caught, you got slugged. She didn't lecture you or say the words that every kid who's gone to school and laughed at a whispered comment has heard, "Well, if it's that funny, why don't you share it with all of us." Sister Edna didn't keep you after school or mete out punishments according to her daily temperament. One detectable laugh simply received one detectable slug.

The part of the day that Sister Edna enjoyed most was Catechism class when she would talk about the "poor souls of Purgatory."

"We must remember, children, each day to pray for the poor souls in Purgatory. It's too late for them to pray for themselves so we are their only hope of shortening their Purgatory time. We must keep in mind that we, too, will some day be poor souls in Purgatory. If we're lucky."

Sister Edna would then tell us about indulgences even though she knew we had been told about them for the past six years. An indulgence was something you could do that would take off Purgatory time either for you or for someone who was already in Purgatory. You could apply an indulgence to whomever you wanted.

Just about everything Catholic could earn you an indulgence. Saying the rosary, making the Stations of the Cross, going to Friday night novena, fasting, and kissing a bishop's ring were just a few of the activities that had indulgences attached to them.

The rules were quite specific about how much indulgence you would get for each activity. Making the sign of the cross, for instance, was good for 150 days off of your, or someone else's, Purgatory time. However, the sign of the cross was worth 300 days if it was made with holy water, a bonus of 150 days just for the holy water.

I once picked up an easy 500 days by kissing a saint's relic. I can't remember now who it was. The relic was a tiny piece of the saint's bone, about the size of a pin head. It was enframed by a purple cloth inside a small plastic case. All I had to do was kiss the plastic case. I felt pretty stupid, but 500 days is 500 days.

The super day for indulgences was All Souls' Day, which fell on November 2. On that day alone, for each set of ten "Our Fathers," "Hail Marys," and "Glory Be's" you said in church, a soul was freed from Purgatory. You could, however, save only one soul per church visitation so you had to step outside of church for a moment in between each set of prayers so it would be considered a separate visitation to church.

On All Souls' Day in sixth grade, Bobby Bracken claimed to have saved over two hundred people. Of course, he lived very close to church. I was never that successful but I did manage to pull quite a few souls out of the fires of Purgatory.

Sister Edna also enjoyed talking about "fallen-away Catholics." "Yes, children, a fallen-away Catholic has lost the gift of faith. He has turned his back on God, and, by his actions, has told God that he does not want to spend eternity with Him in Heaven. A fallen-away Catholic can receive none of the sacraments and therefore stands little chance of ever gaining Heaven.

"Usually, fallen-away Catholics just don't decide one day that they no longer want to be Catholics. It's a gradual thing. They begin skipping their morning prayers. They stop going to Confession every week. They no longer say their rosaries.

"Then, sooner or later," Sister Edna continued to tell us, "weakened by their lack of prayer, they fall into a mortal sin: they deliberately eat meat on Friday or, for no good reason, they skip mass on Sunday.

"After the first few mortal sins, they'll go to Confession to have them forgiven. But after a while, they become hardened to the damning effects of Mortal Sin. They become indifferent to the saving graces that God is sending to them. Eventually, their love of God becomes a forgotten thing.

"I know it's hard for some of you to believe this now, but even among the people in this class, there are probably a few who will eventually lose their faith and become fallen-away Catholics."

Whenever Sister Edna said that, we'd stare at her eyes to see who they were looking at, but they'd always start skipping around, unwilling to tell us who they thought the future infidels might be.

Those Catechism classes were about the only times that Sister Edna's words didn't make too much sense. Who could become hardened to the damning effects of Mortal Sin?

In the middle of the year, Sister Edna started leaving the classroom about every hour for a minute or two. It was very unusual behavior for a St. Bastion nun. They rarely left their classrooms and when they did, they'd normally put their number-one bootlicker in front of the class to take down the names of any kids who looked the wrong way. Sister Edna didn't bother doing that. She didn't have a number-one bootlicker and besides, she wasn't gone for more than a minute or two so there wasn't enough time for any real kind of trouble to start.

Most of us figured she was going to the drinking fountain. There wasn't enough time for her to be going anywhere else. But that didn't make sense, either. The nuns never used the school's drinking fountains. I don't know why. They just never did.

It was a few months after Christmas, in the early part of March, I think. As we came into class that morning, Sister Edna was standing behind her desk, her hands clutching her black knit shawl, which hung loosely from her shoulders. Standing next to Sister Edna was a young nun who had a face that was almost attractive. The young nun certainly came as close to looking good as any nun I've ever seen.

Sister Edna's seven saints, one for each day of the week, were gone from her desk, presumably tucked away in the black briefcase that stood open-mouthed at her feet. The top of the desk was nude save for the twelve-hundred-page book of *Louis, King of France*, which, along with its Saint Joseph holycard bookmark, appeared unmoved.

Sister Edna was busy talking to the young nun. Every now and then, Sister Edna would illustrate a point in her conversation by waving to the blackboards, the window shades, her desk, the coatroom, or by taking out one of the workbooks from her shelf and opening it to a particular page.

Although I couldn't actually hear the conversation that was going on between Sister Edna and the younger nun, I could easily imagine what was being said.

"The blackboards are cleaned every third day, Sister. The girls in each row take turns doing that. . . . I usually pull the window shades down at about two o'clock, especially if I plan on putting any geography questions on the blackboard. Even with the shades down, some of the children can't see the blackboard because of the glare. . . . Each row goes to the coatroom separately and the next row isn't called until the previous one is back and sitting in its seats. . . . Because of the holidays, we're two units behind in our Spelling, but if you take five extra words a week, you should be caught up by the middle of April. . . ."

Our class was undergoing a changing of the guard.

I had seen all of this happen twice before, once in second grade and the other time in sixth grade. It was a case of the nun simply not being able to go the distance and having to get relief help. The nun would be out of school for five or six weeks and then come back with her vicious vitality fully restored.

Usually, the nun who was leaving wouldn't say anything to the class before she left. If some kid asked the new nun where the regular nun went, the new nun would give an answer like, "Sister's gone away to take a little rest," or "Sister hasn't been feeling too well lately so she's gone to stay at our motherhouse for a while to get well," or "None of your business."

After morning prayers, though, Sister Edna did speak to us. "Children, I'm going away for a while and I want you to pray for me while I'm gone." Spoken like a true nun. All nuns want you to pray for them while they're gone. They must think that if you're doing that, you won't have as much time to get in trouble.

"Of course," Sister Edna continued, "I will remember you in my morning and evening prayers and throughout the day." Sister Edna motioned toward the young nun. "This is Sister Gregory, who will be teaching you until I get back. I'm sure you will cooperate with Sister Gregory and make me proud of you."

A girl in one of the front desks raised her hand. She had, through seven years of grammar school, established herself as one of the school's finer bootlickers. As I have mentioned, Sister Edna didn't have any bootlickers but if she did, this girl would have been one of them.

"Sister," the girl asked, "you are coming back, aren't you?"

"I certainly hope so," Sister Edna laughed. "Why? Do you want to get rid of me?"

"Oh, no, Sister," the girl said, "I didn't mean that."

"Does Sister Gregory here look that mean?"

"Oh, no, Sister. . . ."

Sister Edna was just kidding around with her but I don't think the old bootlicker realized it. Sister Edna sure had that kid going.

We all stood and said a "Hail Mary" and an "Our Father" together and then Sister Edna left.

"Man," I thought to myself, "that girl sure did ask a stupid question. Would Sister Edna be back. Was that a stupid question. They all came back.

But Sister Edna didn't. In a month she was dead.

Walking with Lanner through the school yard late at night. Coming back from St. Bastion Church where Sister Edna was being waked. We were almost out of the school yard when I motioned toward one of the concrete blocks.

"Hey, Tom, wanna sit down and shoot the bull for a while?"

"Yeah, sure," he said absentmindedly.

We sat and stared silently at St. Bastion school as she lay anchored on the other side of the school yard. That night, she didn't look like the same overseer who daily sucked me through her doors. Rather, she appeared almost dignified as she floated in the nebulousness of the night, lapping up the wet early spring breeze, her temper cooled by the melancholy mood of the April night.

Lanner and I had spent the past hour kneeling in

front of the open coffin, praying for Sister Edna. The thoughts that have been born there live now in the school yard on the concrete car block.

Neither of us talked but simply sat there, our arms laying across our knees, which were propped up in our faces, each of us tinkering with his own thoughts.

For the first time in its life, my mind began taking a look around: over my shoulder to where I had been, scanning the perimeter to see where I was, glancing ahead to where I might be going.

I had been told before. Hundreds of times. But I never believed it. That night, my mind did reluctantly admit the possibility of its truth. Perhaps I would not be in grammar school forever, I would not be a child, forever. I would not be, forever.

Death. Never before had it burned so closely. Sister Edna was dead. Sister Edna was dead and in that world Father O'Reilly had raved about, that my parents and the nuns had repeatedly told me about, that I had so often thought about. That world of precision judgment and infinite rewards and punishments, of Heaven and the eternal fires of Hell.

The young nun had been called out of our classroom the previous Friday afternoon right after she had handed out the *Young Catholic People's Gazette*. All of us were in our usual Friday afternoon mood, delirious with joy about being within an hour of a weekend.

The *Young Catholic People's Gazette* was a regular part of the Friday afternoon festivities. It was a miniature six-page newspaper, which contained such literary lures as a "Current News" column, a feature story on the "Saint of the Week," two jokes written in dialogue between "Al" and "Nel," a "to be continued" story about either basketball or horses, and an "Open Letters to Father John" column, which contained such Ann Landers questions as "What special graces can I obtain by saying a decade of the rosary before bedtime?"

Since the *Young Catholic People's Gazette* was always handed out on Friday afternoons, it had become the Pavlov bell announcing the weekend. My mouth was already tasting the three o'clock dismissal bell when the young nun came back into the classroom.

There were tears in her eyes. I was fascinated by the phenomenon. I had always thought nuns were limited to two emotions: anger and, more infrequently, sadistic humor. This tear thing was something new altogether. Everyone in the class seemed to be staring in amazement at the young nun.

"Sister Edna," the young nun began speaking sporadically, "passed away this morning at the motherhouse. Her cause of death was bone cancer."

The young nun was speaking so softly that she could hardly be heard. She pulled out a small white-laced handkerchief and began dabbing it around her eyes and nose.

"Sister Edna knew for the past six months that she was not going to live. When the doctors informed her of her condition, Sister Edna simply replied that she was glad it was she and not somebody else who wasn't ready to die."

The young nun continued to talk about Sister Edna, telling us to pray for Sister Edna's soul even though the young nun was sure that Sister Edna was already in the arms of God. I tried to imagine that scene, Sister Edna in the arms of God, but I couldn't. It was just too strange.

After the young nun had finished talking, she walked out of the classroom without saying a word. The room was perfectly still. Not a sound. I looked down at my *Young Catholic People's Gazette*, which was pinned to the top of the desk by my elbows. I had been halfway through the "Open Letters to Father

John" column when the new nun had made the announcement about Sister Edna. I closed the gazette, stuck it in my desk, and put my head down on top of my arms.

Eyelids squashed my eyeballs as I attempted to permanently etch Sister Edna's image in my mind. She was a part of my life that was over and I was afraid that if I forgot what Sister Edna looked like, it would be as if I had never lived that part of my life at all.

The sanctity of the night was shattered by some kids as they walked past St. Bastion school, yelling obscenities at one another. I looked over at Lanner sitting motionless at the other end of the concrete car block.

"What are you thinking about, Tom?"

"Nothing. A lot of stuff."

"About Edna?"

"Yeah," Tom said.

"Me, too," I said. "Don't you wonder where she's at and what she's doing right now and whether she's watching us down here and stuff like that?"

"You know what I think," said Lanner.

"No, what?"

"I think she's watching us and listening to every word we say. And I think she can watch every kid in our class at the same time if she wants to, even if they're all in different places."

"Why do you think she can hear and see us right now?" I asked.

"I don't know. I just kind of think so."

"You mean you sort of feel it, Tom?"

"No, I can't really say that. I just think that's the way it is, I guess."

Silence for a few moments and then.

"I sure wonder what it's like, don't you, Tom?"

"Yeah. We'll find out eventually, that's for sure."

"True enough," I said. "Ever think there might not be a God?"

"Sort of," Tom said. "Yeah, sometimes. You?"

"Sometimes. It must really be something, though. Dying and meeting God, face to face. Having Him talk to you."

"Think you'll get to Heaven, Eddie?" Lanner asked.

"Yeah, I think so. I bet I'll probably have to spend a lot of time in Purgatory, though."

Lanner laughed. "I know what you mean. I don't think I'll be catching the express train, either."

Slivers of rain began slipping from the sky.

"Is it raining?" Lanner held out his hand for a moment and then answered his own question. "Yeah, it is." Neither of us made any attempt to move. "Bone cancer. That's a lousy way to go," Lanner said. "My aunt says you suffer like hell with that."

"You know," I said, "I don't think I would have been able to say 'I'm glad it's me instead of some guy who's not ready to die.' I know I couldn't have said that. I could give a shit for the other guy. Hell, I'll never be that ready."

"Did you see all those five- and ten-dollar mass cards next to Edna's casket?" Lanner asked.

"Yeah. I guess you can take it with you," I said. "Now, what's to stop a guy from stealing millions of dollars and investing them in masses to be said for his soul after he dies? You could steal your way right into Heaven."

"I don't think you could get away with that," said Lanner.

"Why not?"

"I don't know. I just don't think you could."

The rain was gaining strength. "We better get going," said Lanner. "I've got some arithmetic homework I've got to do before I go to bed tonight."

"Think we'll get Wednesday off for her funeral?" I

asked Lanner as I stood up. My rear end hurt from sitting on the concrete block for so long.

"I don't know," said Lanner. "But even if we do get the day off, we'll have to blow the morning going to her funeral mass because we were in her class."

"You're right, Tom. I never thought of that. But I wouldn't worry about getting that arithmetic homework done tonight. Just tell Sister Gregory that you went to the wake tonight. She won't keep you after school with an excuse like that."

"You're right," Lanner said. "If I tell her that, she won't even have me make it up."

Running home. Watching the rain turn the sidewalks tan beneath our feet. Getting out of breath and slowing to a walk as we come to a corner.

"You know, Tom, I kind of liked Edna. She was all right."

"Yeah," said Lanner in between breaths as we crossed the street, "she was all right."

The beginning of a new block. Once again, running toward home.

XIII Eighth Grade: Top of the Bottom

For seven long years, we had heard about it. Older brothers and sisters had told us of its power, its privileges, its pageantry. It was, they said, a year of carefree contentment, chic cosmopolitanism, continuous carousing, and chauvinistic comradeship.

Once you reach it, they said, you will find your tongues speaking a language that only others like you will comprehend. Those younger than you will not understand your ways, for they have not been there. And most of those older than you will have long forgotten that they, too, once walked through the Promised Land.

Depki's older brother, in one of his rare poetic moments, told us just before we began the year, "Never again will so many of you be so goddamn high for so goddamn long." A tear came to his eye as he recalled a personal moment when he was at the peak.

Those older kids were wrong, of course. But after all, they were only finite human beings with limited means of communication. They couldn't help but vastly underestimate the magic of those months that made up the eighth grade.

Like all eighth graders everywhere, we at St. Bastion's were a privileged minority, enjoying a virtual monopoly on all the prestigious positions in the school. The eighth-grade girls monitored the classrooms during lunchtime, ran the school library, and controlled the candy room in the school basement. The eighth-grade boys filled most of the positions on the St. Bastion's football and basketball teams, cleaned the classrooms after school, and were the school's patrol boys.

Every eighth grader, of course, was a school hotshot simply by the fact that he was an eighth grader. But in order to be a hotshot among the hotshots, you had to hold down one of those prestigious positions. In September of eighth grade, it looked fairly certain that God had indeed not chosen me to be a hotshot among the hotshots.

I had absolutely no chance of getting on the football team. To make the St. Bastion football team, you had to have hair on your chest, blood in your eyes, and space in your head.

Father LaBlanca, who coached the team, was a

cross between Knute Rockne and King Kong, with a touch of Bishop Sheen that surfaced at after-dinner speeches. Father LaBlanca consistently produced the best and meanest grammar school football team on Chicago's South Side. Opponents considered it a successful day if they went home alive.

The best way to make the team was to get the word around the neighborhood that you were a stupid, selfish, but savage sonofabitch. Beating up four or five kids right before tryouts would naturally enhance your chances of making the squad. More than one star of Father LaBlanca's was literally snatched from the road that led to the state reformatory.

I was too small to play football for Father LaBlanca. I weighed only about a hundred pounds when I was in eighth grade. Some of Father LaBlanca's players had fingers that weighed more than that. Besides, I was too weak. I never in my life beat up anybody although, throughout my younger years, I was pulverized almost weekly by numerous adversaries. Some of the finest fists in St. Bastion's have pushed through my face.

I could never play basketball very well so I didn't even have to worry about whether I could make that team or not.

Couldn't clean classrooms, either. I'm allergic to dust. Not all dust, just the dust on St. Bastion's floors. Every time I got near that dust, my eyes would swell up like tangerines. I tried sweeping a classroom once and I spent the next three days trying to see through my eyelids.

The only position of power that I was qualified for was patrol boy. Unfortunately, the nun in charge of patrol boys that year was Sister Triona. I had had Sister Triona in sixth grade. On the second day of class, she decided that out of all the seventy-four kids sitting in front of her, she hated me the most. She spent the rest of the year proving it. The next year, Sister Triona was transferred up to the eighth grade and put in charge of the patrol boys.

Being a patrol boy was as close to becoming an adult as you could get. If you were a patrol boy and you said a kid was talking in line, then he was talking in line. If you said a kid was walking too fast, then he was walking too fast. If a kid really annoyed you, you could "bring him up" to the principal, which was something like arresting him. She'd really chew him out or give him a penalty. Sometimes both. Your word was never questioned. It was a great way of life, having absolute power over your peers.

Most of the patrol boys were picked in their last month of seventh grade so that when school opened the following September, they would already know their duties and there would be no confusion. Very few kids were picked for patrol boys once they actually got to eighth grade.

This passing of power from the present eight graders to the future eighth graders was a gradual process. I remember, in my last month of seventh grade, I would be marching along in line through the halls, or outside on the way to dismissal, or crossing a guarded street corner. I would look up, and instead of seeing the eighth-grade patrol boy, I would see one of my own seventh-grade classmates wearing the same granite face of authority and the same white patrol belt as his eighth-grade predecessor.

It was humiliating to realize that he and I were the same age, had identical educational and religious backgrounds, and yet now he was a shepherd while I was still just another lamb among the sheep.

You could tell what television cowboy series a patrol boy watched most often by how he stood on patrol. Back straight, feet apart was a Gene Autry fan.

Thumbs hitched in the belt and head cocked slightly to the left was Roy Rogers. Bowbent back and drooping arms was the Range Rider. When Bobby Bracken, who was a patrol boy, naturally, stood on patrol, he reminded you of Dale Evans.

Like all figures of authority, the St. Bastion patrol boys had a system whereby they could always, whether on patrol or not, be quickly identified as persons not to be messed with. With Chicago cops, it's the Police Association sticker on the windshield. With the St. Bastion patrol boys, it was a wad of white dangling from their waists. After patrol duty, they would roll up their patrol belts into little squares, which they would hang from their pants' belts.

Many were the backs punched in washroom lines. When the victim turned around to retaliate, he would be totally disarmed by a smug smile and a white rolled-up patrol belt dangling from the midsection.

"Blessings often come in strange packages," my mother would frequently tell me. Since it was my mother who told me, I didn't believe it. But she was right. For in eighth grade, I received a blessing in the guise of the worst case of dandruff that world has ever seen.

I don't know where it came from or why, but by the first week of October I had one huge case of dandruff. I tried washing my hair three times a day. It got worse. I tried not washing my hair at all. It got worse. My mother took me to a scalp specialist. "This child has a severe case of dandruff. That will be ten dollars." My dandruff got worse. It got so bad that wherever I walked, it looked like I was leaving a trail of bread crumbs behind me.

"Why don't you get a crew cut," my mother suggested to me one night at the supper table. She had been after me for years to get a crew cut because she thought a crew cut made a kid look clean-cut, neat, and athletic, which were the same reasons why I didn't want to get a crew cut.

There was another reason. I have a very high forehead. If I drew a line across the top of my head from one ear to the other, the line would fall on my forehead. Therefore, I have always combed my hair forward until it's hanging around my nose. It doesn't fool all of the people all of the time but it fools enough of the people enough of the time. With a crew cut, I would be able to fool no one any of the time.

"I don't know, Ma, I don't think I'd like a crew cut," I said as I grabbed for my glass of milk.

"It would allow a lot of fresh air to get to your scalp," my father said to me through the Irish stew in his mouth, "and that's what you need to cure that dandruff. A lot of fresh air up there."

When it came to medicine, my father was a naturalist. By this time I was getting desperate so I reluctantly agreed to get a crew cut.

The next day after school, I got fifty cents from my mother and headed over to Angelo's Barbershop on the corner of 109th and Wendell Avenue.

Neighborhood rumor insisted that Angelo the barber had formerly worked as a hired killer for the Mafia but was forced into retirement when his eyes started going and he began shooting the wrong people. Knowing that Angelo couldn't be happy in a profession where he wasn't drawing blood, his Mafia friends set him up in the barbering business in Seven Holy Tombs.

The tiny silver bell coughed overhead as I pushed open the door to Angelo's barbershop and cautiously walked over to one of his red-vinyl, steel-rimmed chairs. I sat down and began flipping through one of his five-year-old *National Geographic*s, hoping to find some naked breasts even though I knew the odds were against me since I had already gone through each magazine a couple of hundred times.

Angelo had a little body topped by a massive head with ears so large they seemed to stretch out past his shoulder blades. His thick eyebrows hung like awnings over his tiny squinted eyes.

There were about twelve kids ahead of me. Adults never went to Angelo, not even before the holidays. A customer toppled out of the barber's chair, still swooning from Angelo's talcum powder pounding. Angelo pointed to a little kid sitting in one of the red-vinyl, steel-rimmed chairs and, in the same tone of voice that the guard on death row probably uses, said, "You're next."

After the little kid climbed in, his head was about a foot below the back of the barber's chair, so Angelo put in a booster chair. Then Angelo pumped up the barber's chair. Finally, the little kid was sitting high enough for his noggin to be attacked by Angelo.

"Say, how old are you?" Angelo said.

The little kid just hunched his shoulders and sniffled loudly.

"Come on, kid. Are you over fourteen years old? You know if you are, you gotta pay the adult price. Come on kid, how old are ya?"

The little kid held up four fingers. "I'm this old."

"You sure you're not fourteen, uh, kid?"

The little kid nodded his head and then shook it negatively. Angelo grunted and reached for the white sheet, the ends of which he promptly wrung around the little kid's neck.

Angelo then grabbed his electric pearl-handle shears from the shelf behind the barber's chair, threw the button to "on," and swept the shears around the sides of the little kid's head.

Back to the shelf where the electric shears were exchanged for the scissors. A few seconds later, the scissors had completed their assault.

Angelo sprinkled some water on the little kid's head, knocked the little kid's hair down with a comb, made a crooked part, grabbed a large white-fibered shaving brush, threw some talcum powder on it, banged the brush around the little kid's head and face, whipped off the white sheet, let down the chair, tapped the little kid on the head, and said, "Out. Fifty cents."

The elapsed time from the moment of sit-down was slightly under two minutes.

Angelo pointed to another kid and announced, "You're next."

The little kid was still wobbling from the effects of his fast descent in the barber's chair when Angelo walked up to him.

"Fifty cents, kid. Come on."

The little kid jammed his fist into his pocket and fumbled around a moment before yanking the fist out. He slowly opened it, exposing the two quarters on his palm.

Angelo stared at them for a second and then snatched them up. He walked over to the cash register and dropped in the two coins. "A great haircut like that and you don't even tip the barber."

"Huh?" said the little kid.

"Go on. Get going, kid. No loitering around here." Angelo pointed to the No Loitering sign on the wall. "Can't you read?"

"Huh?"

As I sat there in Angelo's red-vinyl, steel-rimmed chair, I tried to convince myself that getting a crew cut was a sane idea. "Well, at least it will cure the dandruff." "I've never had a crew cut before, maybe it will look good." "I guess I haven't got *that* high of a forehead." "What the hell, even if the crew cut does look real bad, my hair grows back pretty fast."

I was so busy talking to myself that I wasn't even concentrating on looking for naked breasts in *National Geographics*.

"You're next, kid." I looked up and saw Angelo pointing at me. Now it was my turn to take that long walk to the barber's chair.

As I hopped up into the chair, Angelo asked, "How old are you, kid?"

"Thirteen, Angelo."

"You look fourteen to me."

I took out a copy of my birth certificate and handed it to Angelo. We had been going through this routine for years. He studied it for a few moments, probably looking for the word "legitimate." Angelo was that kind of guy. He grunted as he handed it back to me.

"Give me a crew cut today, Angelo." I said the words quickly as if speed would make their delivery easier.

Angelo didn't even bothered answering. He just reached for his pearl-handle shears. Angelo was basically a one-bowl barber who produced only one style of haircut, the divot. If he left the hair on top of your head long enough to comb, then it was called a "regular" haircut. If it was too short to comb, then it was a crew cut.

Angelo liked crew cuts almost as much as my mother did. Occasionally, Angelo would get complaints from parents. Too much off the top. Not enough off the top. But there were never any complaints about crew cuts. A few lawsuits perhaps, but no complaints. With crew cuts, Angelo just kept shaving until he hit skin.

As I heard the shears revving up, I said to Angelo, "Make it about an inch high." I indicated the desired height of my crew cut between my index finger and thumb.

ZIP. "Sure, kid, sure," Angelo mumbled as he passed the shears over my head. Ten zips, one water sprinkling, and a talcum powder pounding later, came the tap on the head.

"Out. Fifty cents."

As I slid out of Angelo's chair, I noticed that my head felt decidedly lighter. Angelo didn't have any mirrors in his shop. He figured they might hurt business. Just as well. I didn't trust myself. I was afraid that if I saw what my crew cut looked like in Angelo's barbershop, and I didn't like what I saw, I would either cry in front of Angelo or beat him to death with his own talcum-powdered shaving brush. Neither one would have helped the situation any.

After handing Angelo half a dollar and listening to him complain about the lack of a tip, I took the red knit cap out of my pocket, which had been brought along for the specific purpose of covering up the crew cut on the home flight, and jammed it on my head.

A few times on the way home, I reached under the red knit cap and touched it. I felt kind of fuzzy and certainly, not an inch high. Once, when I reached under and felt it, an old lady was walking by me. She gave me a very weird look.

I wasn't even home yet and already I was beginning to regret the debauchery of my scalp. I could hear my fellow eighth graders exclaiming to one another tomorrow morning when I walked into the classroom. "Gee, I never knew he had *that* high of a forehead."

The girls would shun me and the boys would snicker. Johnny Hellger would make obscene remarks and Lanner would feel sorry for me. And Depki would wonder how I could have been so stupid as to get one in the first place.

As soon as I got into the house I went upstairs to

the bathroom mirror and pulled off the red knit cap. My head looked worse than it felt. Angelo had cut my head so close that it looked like it was covered by a thin layer of swirling dust. Now I knew why my father was so sure that a crew cut would cure my dandruff. You can't have dandruff on a bald head.

My forehead looked big enough to roller skate on. There must have been a foot of skin between my eyes and my hairline. I tried squinching my face to see if I could pull my hairline down any. It helped a little, but not much. I was both enraged and crying at the same time. I went down to the basement to see my mother, who was working on the wash.

From past experience, I knew that if my mother said a haircut looked good, then it looked bad and if she said it looked bad, then it looked good. Her standard of judgment was based on one criteria: length. The shorter it was, the more she liked it. That day I was hoping she'd admit the error of her ways and agree that Angelo had, in ten zips, created a hideous holocaust on my head.

"Hey, Mom, look at my haircut."

"It looks nice, dear."

"Nice! Look at my forehead."

"What's the matter with your forehead?"

"Well, for one thing, there's an awful lot of it, wouldn't you say."

"What are you talking about?"

Just then, I heard my father come in from work. He came down the basement stairs, took a look at my head, and said, "Well, I see you didn't get a crew cut."

"I didn't?"

My mother was waving her hand at him to shut up but he hadn't seen the signal in time and now it was too late.

"If this isn't a crew cut, Dad, then what is it?"

"It's a baldy sour."

"A baldy sour?"

"Yeah, it's the kind of haircut they give you when you go into the army. It's much shorter than a crew cut. It looks pretty good on you." He went upstairs into the living room to hang up his coat.

Baldy sour. It even sounded disgusting.

I got up at about five o'clock the next morning and began dressing for school. I planned on getting to school and into my classroom before anyone else and then hiding my head under my workbooks all day. Then I was going to stay after school and not come home until the entire neighborhood was busy eating supper.

It was still dark when I arrived at St. Bastion school. I pulled on the handles of the big red doors. They were locked. A long time later, as the sun was beginning to trickle over the horizon, came the sounds of someone unlocking the doors. As one of the big doors cautiously cracked open, the head of Sister Triona, the nun who was in charge of the patrol boys, peaked from behind it.

"Mr. Ryan? What are you doing here so early?"

"Nothing, Str. I just wanted to be on time for school this morning."

She pushed open the door a little farther and gestured emphatically with her hand for me to pass by her.

"Come on, come on," she said, "I haven't got all day."

I hurried through the door, past the landing where Sister Triona stood, and began climbing up the school's main steps, which directly faced the big red doors. My feet had eaten up about four steps when Sister Triona's voice froze me from behind.

"Mr. Ryan, come back down here a moment."

I came back down the stairs and stood in front of Sister Triona.

"Something looks different about you this

morning," she said. "Did you get your hair cut?"

"Yes, Str."

"That's a baldy sour, isn't it?"

"Yes, Str."

"I haven't seen a boy wearing a baldy sour in a long long time." Sister Triona glanced up at the ceiling and made a hasty sign of the cross. "My brother, God rest his soul, wore a baldy sour when he was your age. He was a good athlete, you know. Most good athletes wear baldy sours, you know. It makes a man look so clean-cut and healthy, you know."

"Yes, Str."

Sister Triona's mind suddenly came down from the ceiling. "That'll be all, Mr. Ryan."

"Yes, Str." Once again I began climbing up the main stairs and, once again, my ascension was stopped by the voice of Sister Triona.

"Mr. Ryan, come back down here again."

I was in big trouble now. There was no other reason she'd call me back. I must have made too much noise going up the stairs.

Standing in front of Sister Triona, fully expecting to get clouted.

"How would you like to become a patrol boy?"

"Yes, Str, I'd like that." Inwardly I was ecstatic, but outwardly I maintained the same blank expression on my face that one always presents to nuns. It's never a good idea to let a nun know that she's actually communicating with you.

"Go upstairs to my classroom and get one of the patrol belts that are on my desk. Then come down here with it."

Up two flights of stairs and into Sister Triona's classroom, looking for the patrol belts. As I walked into the classroom, my nostrils were immediately infiltrated by that smothered chalk odor that hangs in all cubicles of learning. On her desk were the patrol belts, each one tightly rolled into itself.

I picked up one of the wrapped patrol belts and squeezed it tightly in my hand. Then I tossed the patrol belt up a few inches and let its authoritative weight fall back against my fingers. Symbols of power are always heavy.

When I got back downstairs, Sister Triona was still floating around behind the big red doors, occasionally poking her head out to see if any more students had arrived.

I walked up behind her. "I have a patrol belt now, Str." I held out the patrol belt as evidence.

Her head snapped around to face me. "Well, put it on, put it on."

I unraveled the patrol belt, placed one length of it over my head and the other section around my waist, buckled the belt with its metal clamps, and then pulled on the clamps to make sure they were locked.

Sister Triona gestured toward the top of the stairs. "This morning, you'll stand up there. James Gilmore, who usually has that post, will be absent today. Tomorrow, I'll give you your own assignment."

She began climbing the stairs, taking full advantage of the support provided by the railing. When she reached the first floor, her head turned and squawked over her shoulder, "If any children come while I'm gone, tell them to go directly to their rooms and take out a workbook." Then Sister Triona disappeared down the hallway.

With back arched, I slowly began walking up the stairs, deliberately dropping each footstep and waiting for the ensuing thud to die in the stairwell before dropping another.

Upon reaching the first-floor level, I spun around and stood straight, feet braced far apart, hands clasped behind my back, facing the school's big red double doors, which stood at attention at the base of the stairs.

I had made it. Eddie Ryan, notorious nobody, had become a patrol boy. I silently practiced snapping out orders. Hey, you, quiet. Stay in line. No talking. Pick up those feet. No noise on the stairway.

The first thing that every kid would see when he came into St. Bastion school that morning would be me and my power, my prestige, my . . . baldy sour! I had forgotten all about it.

It was a long morning. Twenty-two hundred came through those big red double doors; twenty-two hundred pairs of eyes bloated in amazement. Twenty-two hundred jaws dropped in awe. And twenty-two hundred minds silently asked, "Who's the forehead at the top of the stairs?"

The next day, Sister Triona put me on the bicycle patrol. It wasn't the greatest assignment in the world but it wasn't the worst, either.

About two hundred kids a day took their bikes to school except when there was heavy snow on the ground. Then the number would drop to one, me. On such mornings, my "snow" tires would swell to five feet in diameter by the time I got to school.

It was my job to make sure kids locked their bikes, didn't talk, and parked them in the right grade section.

Sister Triona said that since I was in charge of the bikes, I should ride a bike to school myself. My own bike had been stolen the year before when I left it at the park so I had to use my sister's bike.

It was a real beauty, with a blue body and all-chrome fenders. My father never walked into a store and bought anything so none of us knew where it came from. He always had a friend who knew of a friend who knew of a friend who knew . . . My father claimed that it was the only bike ever made with pure chrome fenders. I myself have never seen another bike with pure chrome fenders.

Unfortunately, my sister didn't like them. One afternoon, she decided she'd cover them with some orange paint that she had found in the garage. But the paint she had grabbed from the garage shelf was gutter paint, which gets sticky and runs every time it rains. Thereafter, whenever the bike was ridden in the rain, little blips of orange would trail behind it. That orange paint never totally dried.

Being a patrol boy has been one of the few jobs in my life that I have handled professionally. Only one minor incident marred an otherwise flawless performance. On Halloween day of that year, I almost killed a first grader.

It was during lunchtime and, since it was Halloween, I was in a big rush to get home, eat lunch, and get back to school for the Halloween party in the afternoon.

At St. Bastion school, you couldn't dress up like a witch or goblin or anything like that. You had to dress up like one of the saints. I wanted to go to my class's Halloween party dressed as St. Joseph but my mother wouldn't trust me with a hammer. So I went as St. Christopher. You can't do much damage with a globe.

Rushing anywhere on my sister's orange-gutter-painted bike was no minor achievement. It took approximately a thousand pounds of pressure per pedal to get the bike going over three miles an hour.

Racing home to lunch that day, I was doing the best I could. My legs pistoned the pedals as calf muscles ripped away from bone. My tongue, dehydrated from lung exhaust, hung limp from my mouth as perspiring hands slid around the handlebars.

About a half a block ahead of me, I saw a first grader trying to cross the street. First graders are easily recognizable. They are the only ones who have mittens clipped to their coats in October.

As his mother told him to, he was crossing at the

corner and was looking in each direction for oncoming cars. He was within seconds of discovering that his mother didn't warn him about everything.

I was about fifty feet away from him when he started to cross. I began to brake. He saw me coming and stopped. I saw him stop and I started pedaling again. He saw me stop and he began walking again. I started. He stopped. I stopped. He started. I started. He stopped. And then one of my starts hit one of his stops.

I saw him go down in front of my bent bicycle basket. PLUMPLUMP. I got him with both wheels. I jumped off the bike and ran back to him. He was starting to get up, which was a good sign.

"You okay, kid?"

"Sure, I'm okay." He didn't sound too sure. "Did you see my glasses?" he asked.

"Here they are, kid." I picked them off the curb and handed them to him. The lenses were dusty and all but they weren't broken.

"Where do you live, kid?" I thought I'd better walk him the rest of the way home and explain to his mother exactly what happened even though I didn't know exactly what happened.

"Over on 108th and Crandel."

"Okay. Come on, I'll walk you home. You're sure you're not hurt, now."

"Yeah, I'm sure." He sounded a little more convinced of it himself this time.

"Your back doesn't hurt, does it?"

"No."

I had heard my parents talking about how a lot of people involved in accidents liked to sue for phony back injuries so I wasn't taking any chances.

We didn't talk much as I walked him home. What does an eighth grader have to say to a first grader? Nothing. Absolutely nothing.

He was worried about a big blotch of orange gutter paint on his cheek. I told him he didn't have to worry about it because the orange gutter paint never dried, and how the fender dripped when it rained.

"Go ahead," I said, "touch one of the fenders."

"It's sticky."

"See, I told you. It never dries."

I was hoping the kid didn't have any older brothers or sisters that would spread the word in school that I had run him over. I had never heard of a kid getting run over by a bike before. I had heard of kids threatening to run over somebody, but no one actually ever did it. If the word got out that I was running over first graders with my bike, people would think I was a moron or something.

I took the kid up to his house and rang the doorbell. It didn't look like much of a house. The screen on the front door was ripped, the lawn was thinning, and the paint on the house was beginning to peel.

When his mother came to the door, she had on an old housecoat, her hair was in curlers, and she was chewing gum and smoking a Lucky Strike cigarette. Lucky Strikes have a very distinctive smell about them.

"Good afternoon, mam. This is your kid and I just ran him over with my bike."

"Oh yeah, how come?"

"It was an accident, mam."

"I didn't think you did it on purpose."

"No, I didn't, mam."

"You a patrol boy or something?"

I had forgotten about my patrol belt. I still had it on. "Yes, mam, I'm in charge of the bikes."

She took a long drag on her Lucky Strike, took two chews on her gum, and then blew the smoke through her nostrils, which sounded somewhat clogged up.

"You're in charge of the bikes, huh. And you ran over my kid with your bike. Jesus Christ, that's some school they're running over there." The kid was just standing there, listening to all this bullshit.

"I don't think he's hurt, mam."

She opened the screen door, the kid stepped in, and she put her arm around him.

"It's going to take more than being run over by a bike to slow down my Ernest. Last year he was run over by a car and all he got was a bloody nose. This summer, me and my husband took Ernest to a ball game at Comiskey Park and Ernest caught one of Nellie Fox's pop fouls right in the head. Or did Sherm Lollar hit it? Anyway, Ernest hardly missed a bite on his hot dog."

She patted Ernest on his well-worn head. "Me and my husband are very proud of Ernest. He's not very b-r-i-g-h-t but very t-o-u-g-h. Very t-o-u-g-h."

"Well, I have to get going, mam."

She looked down at Ernest again and touched his cheek. "What's this sticky orange stuff on his face?"

"Oh, that's gutter paint, mam."

"Oh."

I don't think the kid had any older brothers or sisters because I never had anyone mention the incident to me. I don't think the first grader told anyone, either. Some friend of his lived right next door to me and he never even asked me about it.

I guess that after getting hit by a car and beaned in the head by a foul ball off the bat of Nellie Fox or Sherm Lollar, getting run over by an orange-fendered bike is, at best, anticlimactic.

XIV *The Sex Talk*

It is part of the American myth that the normal male in this country doesn't become interested in girls until he is well into his teens and doesn't even notice them until he is at least thirteen or fourteen. As every American male knows, such is not the case.

Being an average American male, I experienced my first love affair at the age of four. It lasted three years, one day a year. Her name was Linda Bogan and every year I saw her at the annual Knights of Columbus picnic, which my family faithfully attended.

At each yearly picnic, I would win the footrace and be rewarded with a Sears, Roebuck ukulele and a smile from Linda. I still have all the ukuleles, but I can't say the same for Linda's smiles. In the fourth year, I got off to a poor start in the foot-race and finished second. She would have nothing to do with me. Linda was strictly a first-place girl.

It wasn't until eighth grade, the first week of it to be exact, that St. Bastion Parish and I received our first sex talk. But only years later did I realize that's what it was. During that first sex talk, the word "sex" was never mentioned. And for good reason; it didn't exist in St. Bastion Parish.

The nuns never mentioned it. The closest they ever got to it was during English period when they talked about a noun's gender. " 'He' is of the Masculine Gender, 'She' is of the Feminine Gender." The parish priests never mentioned it. Our parents never mentioned it. The girls never mentioned it.

For eight years, the nuns and priests did tell us about the "Immaculate Conception" of the Blessed Virgin Mary. But like most things the nuns and priests talked about, we had no idea what they were talking about.

Even among us boys, the word "sex" was never spoken. How could we say it? We'd never heard of it. Felix the Filth Fiend Lindor, who could refer to any part of the human anatomy with at least ten different dirty words, never actually used the word "sex."

During the first few years of my existence, I didn't worry that much about where I came from. Occasionally, I'd ask my mother and she'd say, "Why, you came from God. Where else could you come from?"

"How come I don't remember?" I'd ask.

"Haven't you ever noticed how little babies can't talk?"

"Sure I have."

"Well, that's because they still remember Heaven and God doesn't want them to tell anyone about it. As a little baby learns to talk, he gradually forgets Heaven so that by the time he can talk to anyone about Heaven, he's forgotten all about it."

That made sense.

When I got old enough to go to school, the nuns' teachings confirmed my mother's story of my origins. Question 149 of the Baltimore Catechism: WHERE DID YOU COME FROM? ANSWER: I came from God who is all kind, just and good. It was a simple answer. I had a simple mind. I was satisfied.

Eventually, I developed theories of my own that were actually little more than modifications of the original story. For instance, my search for cause and effect drove me to the conclusion that, although I had come from God, I had not come from Him directly. He had dropped me off at the hospital where my mother had to go and pick me up. Keen observation of relatives who had had babies led me to this conclusion. It wasn't until I met Felix the Filth Fiend that I learned the truth of the matter. I learned all the basics from Felix although I'm still learning the finer points.

At St. Bastion school, we could be marching along in line and if somebody got caught goofing off, the nun would take the offender by the shoulder and make him or her stand in the row of the opposite sex.

Our lines were always segregated. Boys made up the right row while the girls stood in the left row.

Being placed in the opposite sex's row by a nun was supposed to cause great embarrassment in the offender. Except for a few people like Felix, who got his giggles by such misplacements, it was quite an effective punishment. Until eighth grade.

We eighth graders were a strange bunch. The girls constantly talked about boys but that was about it. They spent most of their free time watching *Bandstand* on television. Only a few of the girls really mixed with the boys, if you know what I mean. Among us boys, there were those who would, in the same sentence, talk about their sexual achievements and the latest model airplane that they had glued together.

A few years before I started eighth grade, Father O'Reilly had died and Father Myers had been assigned to replace him as pastor of St. Bastion Parish. Father Myers was the first drip in the new wave of liberalism. According to him, you would still go straight to Hell for eating meat on Fridays, but not nearly as fast nor as far down as Father O'Reilly would have had you believe.

In line with this philosophy of liberalism, and knowing that the savage of sensuality was already pacing up and down within us, Father Myers sent Father Vendel, one of the parish's assistant priests, over to St. Bastion school to talk to us eighth graders about the "facts of life," something that had never been done during Father O'Reilly's reign.

When Father Vendel arrived, all of us eighth-grade boys were sent down to an empty first-grade classroom to do our geography homework while the girls were put in one of the eighth-grade rooms to listen to Father Vendel. After he was finished talking to the girls, we were told, he would come down to the first-grade classroom and talk to us while the girls did their geography homework up in their classroom.

As I sat wedged in that first-grade desk, trying to keep my knees out of my mouth as I fought with some fraction, I wondered what Father Vendel was going to say to us. At that point, I had no idea. As it turned out, I had even less of an idea after he said it.

I was kind of excited about just being out of my own classroom. When Father O'Reilly had been pastor, breaks in the daily routine were never tolerated. The only time you were allowed out of your classroom was to go to the principal's office, to the washroom, or for a fire drill.

We were working on our geography homework for about half an hour when we heard the voice of the nun who was watching us boom out from the back of the room. "Close your books, fold your hands on top of the desk, and sit up straight."

Father Vendel sneaked into the classroom, coughed apologetically for being alive, and placed some looseleaf papers neatly on the lectern that he had brought along with him. He was an old priest, built in streaks of lanky flesh, his lean head constantly hovering over his navel.

Ever since Father Myers had made Father Vendel the moderator of the newly formed Teen Club, Father Vendel had felt obligated to keep his gray hair in a crew cut and wear white socks and penny loafers that stuck out obtrusively from beneath his cassock.

Everyone liked Father Vendel because he was a pretty nice guy. I liked him because he was a very sincere guy. I can like anyone who's sincere. He always believed in whatever he was doing even though, most of the time, he didn't know what he was doing, which was another reason why I liked him. I could identify with him.

"Let's stand and say a few prayers, boys," Father

Vendel said, "before we have our little talk. And considering today's topic, I think it would be a good idea if we said a few extra 'Our Fathers' and 'Hail Marys' in asking Our Lord to bless and watch over our discussion."

As we stood up, I heard Depki moan behind me. I didn't know whether he was moaning because of the extra prayers or because he had managed to rupture himself while prodding his body loose from the first-grade desk.

Ten "Our Fathers," "Hail Marys," and "Glory Be's" later, we sat down and squeezed back into the first-grade desks.

Father Vendel first gave us the usual pitch about the possibility of each of us having a "vocation." Whenever anyone at St. Bastion's talked to you about your future, they inevitably mentioned the strong chance of you having a "vocation," meaning God had chosen you to become a priest or religious brother or, if you were a girl, a nun.

Father Vendel informed us that one out of every four of us had a religious vocation and that the only reason one out of every four of us wouldn't become a priest or religious brother was that some of us just weren't listening to God.

He went on to tell us that God had, somewhere in the Gospels, personally promised priests and all other members of religious orders that they would be rewarded one hundredfold in this life, and even more in the next, for whatever sacrifices they made.

I don't think anyone was really listening to Father Vendel, except maybe for a few guys who were debating about going to a seminary high school after they graduated from St. Bastion's. Most of us had already made up our minds about it, one way or the other. We had been getting that same pitch for eight years now.

The nuns were always telling us how being a religious was a higher calling than being a parent. The single life was rarely mentioned and when it was, the nuns subtly suggested that the only ones who remained unmarried were those who refused to answer God's calling them to a "vocation" only to discover that their lives, except for an occasional Sunday dinner invitation, were totally devoid of joy.

I personally couldn't see how the nuns were collecting their one hundredfold but then I saw them only in school. When questioned, many of them insisted they were getting it.

That "vocation" stuff was a very tempting deal. I don't imagine there was ever a Catholic kid who didn't, at one time or another, think of being a priest or a nun. The other alternative, parenthood, certainly wasn't as lucrative as one hundredfold. I was around my parents a lot more than I was around the nuns and I knew, for sure, my parents weren't collecting such dividends.

After Father Vendel finished talking about our "vocations," he picked up one of the loose papers from his lectern and began reading from it.

"Boys, you are at an age when your bodies are undergoing great changes. These changes, like all beautiful and wonderful things, are being brought to you by the infinite wisdom and love of God. These changes, these beautiful gifts of God, are the first steps toward adulthood.

"But the devil, as usual, is jealous of God's gifts to you and is trying to take your souls and condemn them to the everlasting fires of Hell.

"And how is the devil going about this, boys? How is the devil trying to get you to commit a mortal sin and"—Father Vendel interrupted himself to turn to the next page of his notes—"thereby, if you die in the middle of the night without the benefit of a priest's presence, sending your soul to the deepest corners of Hell?

"I will tell you, boys." The next sentence was spoken in an odd mixture of whisper and shout. "By tempting you to commit sins of impurity."

Father Vendel leaned smugly over the lectern, waiting for our faces to blush at the use of such crude terminology. We stared back. Satisfied with himself, Father Vendel went back to reading from his papers.

"First of all, boys, sins of impurity are perhaps the most dangerous kind of sin. Almost all sins of impurity are mortal sins. It is very difficult to commit a venial sin of impurity. Therefore, it is extremely dangerous to commit any sin of impurity.

"Furthermore, boys, it has been estimated that more people go to Hell because of sins of impurity than for any other kind of sin. Perhaps as many as two out of every three people who go to Hell go there because of the sin of impurity.

"Now, boys, you may be asking yourself, 'How does the devil go about tempting me to commit these sins of impurity?' Well, boys, one way the devil always uses is he tries to get us to have impure thoughts. Yes, boys, those impure thoughts are the devil's way of getting you to Hell.

"Remember, boys, that Christ said to His disciples, in Matthew, Chapter 5, Verse 28, 'But I say to you that anyone who so much as looks with lust at a woman has already committed adultery with her in his heart.' Which means, boys, that if you willfully have an impure thought, you are responsible not only for the intention but the act as well."

Sitting there listening to Father Vendel, I knew I was in big, big trouble. My mind spent most of its free time having impure thoughts. And if it was true, as Father Vendel said, that thinking something was as bad as doing it, then I was molesting at least eighty girls a day.

"We must be on our guard, boys, against the devil, who is forever trying to persuade us to attend 'suggestive' movies, look at 'suggestive' books, and associate with 'suggestive' people." Everybody turned around and stared at Felix the Filth Fiend Lindor, but he just maintained his eye fixation on Father Vendel.

"Boys, keep in mind that God realizes you have a lot of excess energy at this age. That is why God allows time for you to play after school, to do homework every night, to help your parents around the house. God wants you to keep busy. A busy young man or woman who is leading a full Christian life doesn't have time for impure thoughts.

"We must constantly remind ourselves that our bodies are made in the image and likeness of God Himself. We are not simply bone and flesh. Our bodies are temples of the Holy Ghost and must be treated as such. Temples of the Holy Ghost," Father Vendel sighed, "isn't that beautiful, boys, to realize that our bodies are temples of the Holy Ghost."

Father Vendel stood there behind his lectern, smiling into his chest and muttering to himself, "Temples of the Holy Ghost, isn't that beautiful." After a few seconds, he came back down to earth, reshuffled his papers, and began reading once again.

"Another way the devil has of getting us to commit sins of impurity, boys, is by tempting us to touch the private parts of our bodies. We should never, I repeat, never never never touch the private parts of our bodies.

"It is a very serious sin, boys, to willfully place yourself in a position whereby you allow yourself to become . . . ah . . . shall we say 'aroused.'

"Sometimes though, boys, through no fault of your own, you will find yourself becoming aroused. You will find yourself having impure thoughts. When that happens, turn to God for help and think beautiful thoughts. Imagine Christ hanging on the cross, dying a torturous death for your sins. Feel the agony of the nails driven through His hands. The unbearable pain of the crown of thorns as they press into His head. Such beautiful thoughts, boys, will save you from becoming aroused and will help you in your fight against sins of impurity.

"Now, boys, I am aware that all of you know individuals who hang around the street corners who consider themselves 'experts' on the topic we have been discussing this morning." Again all our eyes turned toward Felix, giving a silent salute to his raunchiness. This time, Felix recognized our praise. His head hung low over the first-grade desk in order that Father Vendel might not see him. A smutty smile spread across Felix's face while greasy giggles gargled in his throat.

"These so-called 'experts,'" Father Vendel continued, "actually know very little of what they are talking about. Worse yet, they try, by their 'snide' and 'cute' remarks, to make the beautiful God-created relationship between man and woman a dirty and disgusting thing.

"But remember, boys, our bodies were not created to be made fun of or to be ashamed of. They are temples of the Holy Ghost. Isn't that beautiful, boys, temples of the Holy Ghost."

Father Vendel then had a movie projector rolled into the classroom. For the next twenty minutes we were subjected to a color version of "The Life Cycle of the Polar Bear."

"Now, boys," Father Vendel shouted over the whine of the projector as it rewound the film, "are there any questions? None, uh. Well, uh . . . ."

Father Vendel was just stalling around. It was customary that, after a priest had spoken to us, one of the bootlickers would ask him if he would give us his blessing. A priest considered it extremely poor taste not to be asked for his blessing.

The nun in the back of the room coughed loudly. Finally, Bobby Bracken raised his hand.

"Uh, yes? Bobby," Father Vendel said.

Bobby Bracken stood up. "Could we have your blessing, Father?"

"Why certainly. Kneel down, boys."

We pried our bodies loose from the first-grade desks and plopped to the floor on our knees. Father Vendel muttered some Latin and waved his hands over us a few times in the sign of the cross. We stood up, mumbling, "Thank you, Father," and began lining up at the door.

"Now remember, boys," Father Vendel said as we began marching out of the classroom, "your bodies are temples of the Holy Ghost."

When we got back to our own classroom, it became quickly apparent that Father Vendel had told the girls a few things that he hadn't bothered telling us boys. As we filed into the room, every girl looked up from her geography homework and gave us a facial expression normally reserved for a newly arrived pile of manure.

It seems that Father Vendel had told the girls it would be a good idea to stay away from boys since all of them, without exception, had very dirty minds.

XV *Finale*

Then came the month of June and God handed us a deed to the world. Every song that was played on the radio seemed to be written for us, the eighth graders of St. Bastion's. When adults met, they spoke only of us. Every story line of every television show had only us in mind. The sun rose only to shine on our heads.

The latest dance step bounced from our feet, graduation ribbons flowed from our chests, dry wit dripped from our mouths, and visions of the future glistened in our eyes. We were, in the words of Felix the Filth Fiend, truly hot shit.

St. Bastion school continued to exist, of course, but only for our glorification. We were positive that the school would disintegrate behind us once we had stepped out its doors for the final time. Our days of diagraming sentences were indeed just about over.

That June, we went through our last year-end Workbook Push. In all my years of grammar school, no nun ever managed to pace her class fast enough to get all their workbook pages done by the end of the school year. So during the last few days of school, the nun would have us do nothing but workbook pages for five hours a day. As soon as all the workbooks were completed, they'd be put into stacks and carried down to the principal's office by some of us boys.

The nun would always tell us that we wouldn't be able to go on to the next grade the following September unless we finished all our pages. She'd also inform us that the principal would spend all summer going over every page of every workbook of every kid in the entire school.

It was an established fact, however, that as soon as we kids left the school on the final day of class, all the nuns would go to the principal's office and carry all the stacks of workbooks down to the school basement where they were then promptly thrown into the school furnace and burned.

During our final days of eighth grade, the nuns would try to burst the bubble with the infamous comment, "You may be at the top of the pile now, but just wait until next year when you get to high school. You'll be right at the bottom of the heap again."

"Next year." They had to be kidding. No eighth grader ever thought of "next year."

On Graduation Day, the nuns turned away four girls who showed up for the ceremony in sleeveless dresses. For the next three months, Bobby Bracken insisted that sexual intercourse had something to do with a girl's biceps.

Our class behaved in the traditional Graduation Day manner. The girls cried while the boys laughed like madmen.

A couple of weeks before we were to graduate, Johnny Hellger, Tom Lanner, and a few other guys were caught stealing out of the Church's poor box. I'm sure Johnny Hellger talked Lanner into it. All of them caught royal hell. The fact that there wasn't a kid in the parish who had more of a claim to some of that money than Lanner never entered into it.

The weeks following Graduation Day contained the filet of the eighth-grade finale: the graduation parties. Such parties couldn't be held before graduation because the nuns wouldn't allow it. They defined an orgy as any social gathering where both sexes attended.

Teddy Baskin's party was a good one. Teddy was built like a half-melted ice cube. His face was smeared with freckles, his nose constantly ran, and he had a beer belly even though he didn't drink. Yet, he was the most popular boy among the eighth-grade girls.

Teddy was a devout patron of the portable radio. He had no faith in transistor radios, which were relatively new then. He spent most of his time waddling along the sidewalks of the neighborhood, his left arm wrapped around his blaring portable radio, which looked big enough to be a floor model. The fingers on

Teddy's free hand snapped out the tune while his head and rear end swung in opposite directions to the beat of the music.

If you passed Teddy on the street, he'd smile and wave and you'd return the salute. No point in saying hello as Teddy had gone deaf years ago. He'd been walking around like that since third grade. For five years, he was considered nuts. But by eighth grade, he was considered "in."

With all his smiling and waving, Teddy made a lot of friends, especially among the girls, so his party was a big success.

I almost didn't go to Teddy's party. My fingers, on their usual morning pimple patrol, felt a huge one just about to surface on my chin. I couldn't quite see it yet, but I could really feel it.

Only after Johnny Hellger assured me that Teddy's basement was as dark as a dungeon did I decide to go to the party. I had a great time. But it was a good thing for me the basement was dark because it was the kind of party where a pimple would have really stuck out.

Gloria Downgill also had a good party. It could have been a lot better if she had listened to Felix Lindor. Twelve times he suggested that we play "Spin the Bottle" or "Post Office" and twelve times she pretended she didn't hear him.

Gloria Downgill was one of those girls who hits her social peak in eighth grade and then is never seen or heard of again. In seventh grade, she wore her hair short and straight. But the sheet of hair hanging off the left side of her head looked a lot longer than the sheet of hair hanging off the right side of her head. She wore her glasses crooked, too. Maybe Gloria Downgill thought that made her haircut look more balanced.

The miracle occurred right at the beginning of

eighth grade. One day Gloria Downgill was ugly and the next day she was gorgeous. I don't remember exactly when it happened. But it did.

She immediately became the girl to be seen with. She formed a clique of friends that virtually monopolized the eighth-grade social scene.

Tons of kids came to her party, which roared far into the night, right up to the eleven o'clock curfew when everybody had to go home.

But within a year, the peach of St. Bastion's eighth-grade class began to rot. Two years later, she looked little better than a rusted pit.

The cycle had been completed. Not that Gloria Downgill looked the same as she had in seventh grade. But she looked just as ugly, only in a different way.

I suspect that today, somewhere, she is standing behind a sales counter or on top of two little kids in some miniature two-room apartment. And nary a day is allowed to dissipate that the mind of Gloria Downgill doesn't drift back to those ecstasies of eighth grade.

XVI SWANK

I squint to see the dials on my watch: 4:30. Better get going if I want to catch that plane tonight. The sun is just beginning to die. I shiver from the cold death air as it settles on the day. A yellow autumn sky glows above Seven Holy Tombs Park as the sun winks over the horizon.

The young mothers with their baby carriages are home now preparing dinner. A few old men remain on the park benches but most of them, too, have surrendered the park to the neighborhood kids.

Walking down Wendell Avenue to catch a bus on the main street that will take me out of Seven Holy Tombs.

I let the first bus go by. It's an express that runs directly out of the neighborhood. Waiting for the local that winds around a few additional streets before it leaves Seven Holy Tombs. On one of those streets is a friend I'd like to catch a glimpse of before I leave.

My father wanted a pack of cigarettes. I think that's the reason we stopped. The drugstore we pulled up to was on the corner of 109th and Talson, "Sin Corner" of the world. The rest of the family was talking about the Aunt Reggie dinner they had just endured, the final point of which proved nothing but the limits some people will go to for a topic of conversation on a late Sunday afternoon.

I simply stared out the back window at a mystic structure across the street, pushed twenty feet back from the sidewalk and caught between Elmwood Cleaning on one side and Henry's Pizza House on the other. Across the top of the building was a huge metal billboard with a man and a woman skating like they do in the Olympics and above them, in blatant orange letters, was SWANK Roller Rink.

Although I had heard a lot about the SWANK I had never actually seen it. The yellow-tinged brick wall with its blob orange steel doors seemed to indicate a greater life in the thereafter but my fourth-grade mind could not even begin to comprehend what actually lay beyond. It was after Sunday closing time and the crowd had by now slithered back to their dens.

As the car pulled away, I swore to myself, "I shall return, and soon." The SWANK just sat back, looking aloof and very very tough. I was wrong. It was quite a while before I got in there.

SWANK Roller Rink, besides being the bar mitzvah of the neighborhood, was also its class structure. If you were a connoisseur of the SWANK, you were most assuredly bourgeois, but if you didn't frequent that cathedral of wooden wheels, you were strictly a peon. And I, at the age of nine, realized that I was, in fact, a peon.

Within a year, Johnny Hellger had become a frequenter of the SWANK. Not only had he become a rookie of such a place at the tender age of ten but he had also, so he claimed, skated with Pat Redglen, *the* sex symbol of all time. She had a very sinister smile that was quite appealing. I never met her but she had that smile in a picture Johnny Hellger had of her. He told us that he even went to the show with her and they kissed every time the actors did on the screen. I never wanted to do anything like that, though. With my luck, I would have gone and drawn a straight run of Bugs Bunny cartoons.

If you want to know the truth, my parents and Johnny Hellger's played in a different league. Going somewhere with Redglen was just inconceivable for me, so why dream?

He being a rookie, Johnny Hellger went only on Saturday mornings. As soon as the morning session had ended, he'd come over to the street corner where the rest of us had been playing softball. Nothing could break up a softball game faster than a Johnny Hellger fresh from the SWANK Roller Rink.

We'd stand around him while he'd tell us about the beautiful women, the flashing of the colored lights, the roar of the organ, the violence of the foxtrot. Then, all of a sudden, Johnny Hellger would say, "Hey, I've got better things to do than stand around here and shoot the bull with you guys," and he'd walk off. Man, we could just imagine the "better things" a guy like Johnny Hellger had to do.

After he had gone, the rest of us would just sit around. We wouldn't even talk or anything. I mean, here we had been knocking a stupid softball around the street while at the same time the lurid life of the SWANK was going on only a mile and a half away. Fox-trot? We didn't even know what it was.

By the time I reached the seventh grade, I had become a regular attender of the SWANK Saturday morning sessions, the first apprentice step in becoming a full journeyman of the SWANK. The simple fact that these rounds went on inside the SWANK made them mystery beads in one's rosary of life. But outside of that, they were strictly passé.

For one thing, Saturday morning sessions were overpopulated with Boy Scouts, Girl Scouts, and all other sorts of weirdos. Such organizations in my neighborhood gave out merit badges to anyone who could prove that they couldn't stand on roller skates any longer than three seconds. Their leader was always some stocky little log-legged chunk who skated like she had no knees.

Saturday morning didn't even have live organ music. It was taped. The highlight of the session came at about ten-thirty when the race was held, the prize being a ticket to the next week's morning session.

What they'd do is line up all the little guys at the starting line and then they'd take the two social retards who were obviously big and good enough to be skating at the afternoon session and put them all the way on the other side of the rink, about eighty yards behind the rest of the mob, in order to make the race fair. Sure it was.

As soon as the whistle blew, the mob inched forward, bodies self-destructing all over the place. The ones who didn't fall out of ineptness succumbed to sheer panic as they heard those two huge morons behind them building up speed like madmen. You'd look over your shaky shoulder and you'd see two low-crouched forms, arms swinging, legs pumping, eyes like laser beams heading straight for you. Swish swooish swooish Swish swooish swooish Swish swooish swooish kill! kill! kill!

Within seconds after the race began, the two morons would reach the crowd and begin playing Sherman's "March to the Sea," the first one bouncing to the floor any bodies that had managed to remain intact, the other guy cutting around the front of the pack to take the lead.

The two usually glided the last hundred yards quite nonchalantly, no longer in the crouched positions of challengers but in the upright and dignified forms of champions, readjusting the collars of their blue denim shirts like all goons after a successful hit. A few deteriorated minds would cheer them as they crossed the finish line. Probably the same ones that backed the Yankees when they came to town.

The rink was almost silent then except for an occasional moan from one of the fallen. The floor looked like a battlefield, bodies strewn all over the place. The air was thick with the odor of fresh blood and broken dreams. Why, some of the fallen had practiced hours just to get run over. No doubt about it. Boy Scouts are born losers.

The Saturday morning sessions served their purpose, though. They transformed me from a stumble-two, skate-one, love-your-mother, stay-near-the-railing, be-polite sucker to an elbows-out, shoulders-in, speeding, cutting, compulsive, get-out-of-my-way-or-I'll-skate-over-your-head, eight-wheeled maniac. I was ready for the afternoon session.

In the late 1950s, Frankie Avalon was singing "Venus, if you will, please send a little girl for me to thrill . . . ," Eisenhower had the nation safely tucked in bed, the New York Yankees and the Church were still infallible, Vietnam was the name of an Oriental dish, and I was going to the Saturday afternoon sessions at SWANK Roller Rink. Camelot it was!

To try and imagine the exhilaration of skating three hours at the SWANK on a Saturday afternoon is beyond man's mere mind. "Eyes have not seen nor ears heard . . ."

The mere physical beauty of the SWANK was overwhelming. The rink itself was made of the purest oak plywood imported from Gary, Indiana. The surface was as smooth as Lincoln's face and the entire thing was covered by a thin, yet very penetrating layer of dust so that if some ding-a-ling fell, his point of contact was marked by this indelible mist that stigmatized him for the rest of the session. It also served as ample warning to others of their fate if they chose to be clods.

In the middle of the rink an oval had been drawn. If you wanted to skate backward during an "all-skate," you had to do it inside this oval. The oval was also the home base for the SWANK guards, a group of sweat-soaked, fatty-faced bums, naturally all natives of Seven Holy Tombs, who had dropped out of school at about the third grade or as soon as they could count to eight in order to know if all their wheels were there. They weren't.

When someone would fall, one of these guys would race out of the oval with all the finesse of a jackhammer, knocking over at least a dozen people on his way to helping the poor slob who probably had been rollered to death already anyway.

Directly above the center of the rink, about fifty feet up, hung a silver sphere the size of a basketball, that constantly twirled. When the colored lights began flashing on and off, the sphere would catch flecks of them and flick the fragments across the ceiling, turning the entire SWANK into a kaleidoscope.

The colored lights, which had never been taken down from SWANK's first Christmas party, did not contain a psychedelic message but rather one of power. They were overloading SWANK's electrical system and that's why they kept flashing on and off.

The walls of SWANK were two-tone; the upper half being a Puke Purple, so called because it could cause or cover up said fact depending on whether it was instigator or victim. The lower half being Wolski Red, named after its creator, Arthur Wolski.

Running alongside the actual skating area was a skate room that was always good for a few broken kneecaps since some joker who was looking at something he really shouldn't have been looking at would inevitably skate into one of the low-lying benches.

Next door to the skate room was Sarah's Snack Bar. Sarah looked forty, acted twenty, and talked like she was ten. The rumor was that Sarah had tried to be a neighborhood whore but things hadn't gone her way. In an area of the city where 95 percent of the population was under thirteen, it wasn't hard to figure out why.

Sarah wasn't too terribly bright either. She never did learn how to mix the Coke syrup with the soda water. Her gummy Cokes would stick to your teeth like Milk Duds. There was also something very strange about her ice cream bars that I never have been able to figure out. I'd just about get the wrapping off and it would be melted all over my hand. It was very odd.

After Sarah's Snack Bar came the dance room. It was where all the "scancs" hung out. A "scanc" was a not-too-nice term to apply to a girl. Although no one could actually define a scanc, all but the simplest of souls could spot one. Her hair was ratted, she wore very tight black slacks that had creases going sideways, used makeup, and tied her babushka directly on her chin as if it were a riot helmet instead of a babushka.

They had a jukebox in the dance room and all these crazy girls would dance in there for almost the entire session. The only time they'd put on their skates would be for the "ladies only" number. Really. At about a quarter to three, ten minutes before the "ladies only" number was to come on, all these girls would start putting on their skates. They'd go out and skate the "ladies only" and then come right back and dance the rest of the afternoon. I suppose this custom worked on the same principle as closing a private road once a year that's normally used by the public. If you don't do something occasionally, people are going to think you can't do it at all.

Then there was the washroom. Anyone who used the SWANK washroom did so because of one of several reasons: he had had one too many of Sarah's Cokes; he possessed no kidneys whatsoever; he was a narcissist and had to comb his ducktail just one more time; or he had never been to the SWANK before.

The air in there was ninety proof, a mixture of Vitalis, H A Hair Arranger, Brylcreem, and Vaseline Hair Tonic for men plus a healthy dose of that gas exclusively produced by forest-preserve outhouses. It would have been a great place to train scuba divers. No one ever inhaled twice. Not twice.

To get to the SWANK washroom, you had to travel down two steps, on skates. You would have to hold on to the wall and go down them very gingerly, as if you were stepping into a pool of ice water.

Immediately after the steps, you have to make two quick ninety-degree turns. Miss the first turn and you'd cut your midsection in half on one of the sinks. Miss the second and you'd skate right into a toilet. Usually, a ten-minute wait was in order since half of the facilities were stuffed up and overflowing.

For me, it was a very nervous ten-minute wait. If I perchance bumped into one of the ducktails, he'd get very touchy about it. He had to. It was part of his code of ethics. He'd say something like, "Hey, asshole, don't you know how to skate?" I had to mumble something back. It was part of my code of ethics. I suppose I could have told the jerk the truth. "Sure I do, but not in two feet of water while holding my breath for ten minutes." Then the ducktail would say, "Okay, wise guy, see you outside after skating's over."

The rest of the afternoon would be spent in visions of being mauled in front of SWANK viewed by an audience of girls I had tried to impress during the last ten years of my life. The guy would never show up but it was certainly a wear on the nerves.

Once I dreamt that I had actually fallen in the SWANK washroom. I've never even heard of someone falling in the SWANK washroom. What would someone do who did fall in the SWANK washroom? Who would he talk to? Where would he go? How would he get home? What would he do when he got home?

The last landmarks at SWANK were the organ nest and, directly above it, a light board that flashed the name of the dance number in progress. In one corner of the board was a small red light, which beamed only when the fox-trot ritual was being performed.

The organ nest hung out like a tree branch over one corner of the rink. It was more profanely known as "Lloyd's Limb." Lloyd, the organist, had this very long vulture face, clawlike fingernails, a kind of protruding nose, and wore his hair in a style that suggested he never went to the barber his mother sent him to when he was a kid.

When you were skating around the floor, you had an instinctive aversion to going near Lloyd's Limb.

You kept getting the feeling that at any moment Lloyd was going to leap off of his perch, sweep down, and grab you by his clawlike fingernails and deposit you in some ungoldly place, like the washroom.

Rumor had it that Lloyd's mother suffered from delusions of grandeur. She'd figured that Lloyd was going to end up in Carnegie Hall. But one thing that worked against Lloyd's claim to fame was his ability to remember music. He couldn't. It took him literally years to get one song down. By 1958, he was just wrapping up "Paper Doll."

But Lloyd could really play the boogie-woogie, the national anthem of all roller rinks. Lloyd only played the boogie-woogie for important occasions like the fox-trot, a dance in which the guy skated as fast as he could backward while dragging a girl along with him who happened to be skating forward, if all was going well.

The fox-trot was easily the most violent moment of any session save the Saturday morning one, which didn't have any fox-trot mainly because anyone who was skating backward on Saturday morning was probably doing so involuntarily.

Although there weren't many things Lloyd could do to perfection, he could play loud and long. Loud? If Lloyd wasn't in full view, you'd swear to God he was leaping on the keys. And long? In all the years the SWANK was open, no one ever saw Lloyd not playing the organ. Put them all together and you had a very loud and long boogie-woogie.

Skate a boogie-woogie on Saturday afternoon with Lloyd at his machine and the boogie-woogie would be hanging on your ear lobes till the following Friday. There were some weekly worshipers who existed in a perpetual audio world of boogie-woogie.

Every Saturday afternoon, at a quarter to two, I'd head out for Tom Lanner's house, skates slung over my shoulder in appropriate pony express style. We'd head up the main street, past St. Bastion school, the park, through the business district, and alongside the cemetery hill, shooting the bull all the way.

The first "all-skate" of the afternoon would be spent looking for a chassis to drag around in the upcoming "couples only." As soon as an acceptable one was spotted, not so cute that she'd turn me down nor so ugly that she'd turn me off, I'd start skating within her vicinity so that once the "couples only" flashed on the big board over Lloyd's Limb and the great dome of the rink darkened, I would be able to glide up to her and garble, "Would you like to skate?"

My social consciousness extended to the point of knowing about deodorant. Mouthwash was a good year off. The only Freudian insight I got out of such affairs was that if one goes around with an unknown girl, especially in a roller rink, his hands will get sweaty.

After the "couples only" I'd look around for Lanner and we'd slide around the rink during the "all-skate." One did not stay with a girl after a "couples only." Such was paramount to a formal proposal of marriage, or more.

As 4:30 approached, the kill-free attitude of the SWANK was slowly swallowed up by an apprehension that perhaps 4:30 would never come. Maybe it wouldn't be as great as the last one. What if the world really did end this time?

Up to 4:30, everything was strictly preliminary. "Couples only" were for kids and "waltzes" for lovers. But at 4:30 came the orgasm of the SWANK Roller Rink—the fox-trot. And that was only for the pros.

On that great board in the sky would suddenly flash those horrendous words, FOX-TROT. It was every man's high noon. Did he have what it takes to go out

221

there, in other words no brains, or would he choose to stand along the sidelines smiling blandly and hoping everyone would think he had a bad back that he was too proud to talk about. But the fox-trot was a lot like quicksand: stand around it too long and you were bound to fall in.

The couples are out there now. A few girls, just seeing the board, realize that they are not out there for a waltz but for THE FOX-TROT and they can't get the madmen to let go of them. Old Lloyd is warming up with some 1930 tune waiting for that red light, the checkered flag of the fox-trot, to flash on.

RED! Hips jutting, skates slicing out as the couples build up speed. Boogie-woogie boogie-woogie boogie-woogie boogie-woogie. There's a couple down. Another one piles into them. A third one hits both of them. Here come two guards like Mack trucks on a puppy farm. They knock over three more couples. Boogie-woogie boogie-woogie boogie-woogie boogie-woogie. A girl passes out. Her partner keeps dragging her on. He doesn't even know it. Another couple has made the mistake of looking up at the silver sphere. Damn rookies. They're both hypnotized . . . heading straight into a . . . boogie-woogie boogie-woogie boogie-woogie boogie-woogie.

Lloyd's in the homestretch. His fingernails look as if they're going to touch the ceiling the instant before he plunges them into the keys. Lloyd's face looks like the hot end of a thermometer and the sweat's creating creases in his cheeks. The Puke Purple and Wolski Red walls balloon out with every blast and like all great outfielders reaching over the fence for the home-run ball, grab that boogie-woogie and fling it right back to Lloyd. And caught in the crossfire are those skates-screaming, torso-twitching, face-flushing leg-lashing, sphere-spinning boogie-woogie boogie-woogie boogie-woogie boogie-woogie kids.

It stops. The Puke Purple and Wolski Red walls shudder as if suddenly conscious of what they have come through, sigh, and relax.

Lloyd has bounced into a jazz version of "Chattanoogie Shoe Shine Boy." No one's ever heard of Chattanoogie or a shoe shine boy for that matter but they know it marks the end.

The red light flickers off both on the board and in Lloyd's complexion. He looks almost normal now. As close as he'll ever get. The guards are still growling but their breathing isn't quite as heavy and their fangs are almost covered.

Still everyone skates. Admirers begin shouting from the sidelines, "It's over, it's over." But those fox-trot veterans hear only one sound in that cubicle that previously housed a mind. Boogie-woogie boogie-woogie boogie-woogie boogie-woogie.

Finally they come off the floor, disdainful of those who gather about them. Their eyes glare through these parasites with their friendly pats and hollow words of praise.

"Where were you when the big one came? Where were you when the chips were down and the boogie-woogie was up? Where were you?"

Within a few minutes, Tom Lanner and I were on our way home, our feet reluctantly readjusting to the law of gravity. It was about five-thirty now and as the sky squeezed out the sun, Tom and I would walk alongside the cemetery hill, down the main street, through the business district, and on home talking about very important things, which like all important things have long since been forgotten. We were in no big rush to get home and our pace gave evidence. Contented people don't walk very fast.

As they usually do, the years slipped between the SWANK and me until their weight wedged us apart and we went our separate ways.

I worked for a few years in downtown Chicago and every day I would drive right past the SWANK. I never thought about it much. You tend to take old friends for granted. Since then, I've heard that she's closed a few times but it didn't bother me one way or the other. Who doesn't rest when they get a little older?

Riding along in the bus, searching through my wallet for my plane reservation. The bus stutters to a stop at a corner. I look up.

She is dead. Already her left side has been leveled and where the silver sphere once hung stands a crane with its lead wrecking ball mimicking the past. Sarah's Snack Bar is where we're all heading and the organ nest is empty. Lloyd's Limb without Lloyd. Good God!

Looking at those sun-embarrassed Puke Purple–Wolski Red walls in their crippled condition empties me. I don't know why I am so surprised. Real hearts aren't candy-shaped and rosy-colored.

Finally the bus turns and crawls through the intersection, down the main street, through the business district, and over the cemetery hill where Lanner lies.

As I jostle along in her lit-up belly, the bus's wheels seem to mumble incoherently, slowly, boogie . . . woogie . . . boogie . . . woogie . . . boogie . . . woogie.